Principia Ponderosa

Third Flatiron Anthologies
Volume 6, Book 18, Spring 2017

Edited by Juliana Rew
Cover Art by Keely Rew

Principia Ponderosa
Third Flatiron Anthologies
Volume 6, Spring 2017

Published by Third Flatiron Publishing
Juliana Rew, Editor and Publisher

ISBN #978-1544038285

Discover other titles by Third Flatiron:
(1) Over the Brink: Tales of Environmental Disaster
(2) A High Shrill Thump: War Stories
(3) Origins: Colliding Causalities
(4) Universe Horribilis
(5) Playing with Fire
(6) Lost Worlds, Retraced
(7) Redshifted: Martian Stories
(8) Astronomical Odds
(9) Master Minds
(10) Abbreviated Epics
(11) The Time It Happened
(12) Only Disconnect
(13) Ain't Superstitious
(14) Third Flatiron's Best of 2015
(15) It's Come to Our Attention
(16) Hyperpowers
(17) Keystone Chronicles

License Notes

www.thirdflatiron.com

Contents

*****~~~~~*****

Editor's Note

by Juliana Rew

Welcome to the Ponderosa, land of wide-open spaces and dark pines. Wikipedia defines **Weird West** as a literary subgenre that combines elements of the Western with another literary genre, usually horror, occult, fantasy, or science fiction. The seventeen authors of this anthology dig into the principles that have made the Old West and Victoriana such rich ground for speculative fiction and adventure. Let the mining begin.

Such an anthology would not be complete without a steam-powered zeppelin or two. *Principia Ponderosa* leads off with "Blazing Beamard," by Stanley Webb, in which we discover that a formidable dragon is really a coal-fed monster put to work raiding trains for their gold. "The Great Man's Iron Horse" by Mark Mellon introduces another ground-devouring invention that threatens to drive the railroads out of business. But new inventions can't solve every problem, as we see when a lumbering machine becomes the peacemaker in Philip DiBoise's "Closing the Frontier."

As you expect, there are a lot of trains. Trains that built the west, and transported a strange assortment of denizens, both living and spectral, to their proper destinations. In Salinda Tyson's "The Hunt," an avenging eco-spirit decides enough is enough and changes the hearts of hunters shooting buffalo from trains for sport.

A lovely bit of magical realism worms its way into our psyches when a bunch of outlaws ride into the town of "Mourning Dove" by Jackson Kuhl, only to find their fates predicted in the morning paper.

Do not forsake me, oh, my darling. You've been challenged to a gunfight at high noon in front of the saloon, and it's pouring rain. Why haven't you gotten out of Dodge? A great new entry from Martin M. Clark is "No County for Young Men," a slow build to an explosive duel fought with particle beam sidearms.

A thread running through many of the stories is justice for women in the old west. The scream of a woman starts the action in Robert Walton's Gold Rush tale. Should the men rush to her aid, or will "La Loca" take care of business? In "Lampblack and Dust," J. L. Forrest's witch summons her moving tattoos to rescue her protégé, in a tale reminiscent of Vonda McIntyre's *Dreamsnake*. The steampunk heroine tends to be strong too, as we see in John J. Kennedy's "The Gleaming," as she overcomes the loss of an arm to become the first bionic woman.

The solitude of the lonely prairie sometimes plays tricks with the imagination, so we include a taste of horror in this collection. Premee Mohamed's practical farm family is used to losing stock to the harsh conditions of the farm, but they also have to be "Willing" to sacrifice even further to ensure a good harvest. Jordan Ashley Moore's retired sheriff revisits the scene of an unsolved murder in "The Quiet Crime"—unable to forget how the killer simply vanished into thin air.

Appearances can be deceiving, as we see in Columbkill Noonan's "The Groks of Kruk County," a hilarious tale of drug-addicted mountain folks who end up dead, but keep up their haunting ways even though people see right through them. In Angus McIntyre's "The Monster Hunter," we wonder how he can keep killing monsters that everyone is pretty sure are imaginary.

Anchoring the collection is Geoff Gander's powerful chiller, "The Wind Father." Homesteaders are brutally murdered, but when Canadian Northwest Mounties investigate, instead of a frontier conflict, they encounter an entity thirsting for power—and human blood.

To lighten the mood, we close as usual with our "Grins and Gurgles" flash humor section, with pieces by

Lisa Timpf ("Dealing with the Ship's Cat"), Sheryl Normandeau ("Gardening in a Post-Apocalyptic World"), and Brian Trent ("The JPEG of Dorian Gray"). Hmm, does it seem like our northern authors have a lock on humor?

We're happy this time around to have discovered some great new writers, It's gratifying to feature and encourage budding talent. We hope you'll thoroughly enjoy these sagas, told by an international group of excellent storytellers. Saddle up and ride with us into the sunset.

*****~~~~~*****

Blazing Beamard

by Stanley Webb

Soot hovered on the desert scrub.

Special Agent Bull Wire said, "Ease off the throttle, Smokey."

The train driver complied. "My name's Stanislaw."

The smoke built, layer upon layer, until it smothered Bull's locomotive. The headlight cast a sickly, red glow. The men pulled their wild rags over their noses. Suddenly, broken rails appeared. Stanislaw pulled the brake.

Bull jumped to earth. "Follow me, Smokey."

Stanislaw muttered a curse.

A caboose, burned down to its flatbed, appeared through the murk, then incinerated freight cars. The passenger cars bore naught but greasy ash.

The iron vault car sat on broken axles, its plating sprung, and the gold shipment missing.

Bull growled, "What sort of man are you, Beamard?"

Stanislaw spat. "A murderer in need of hanging!"

"He needs worse than hanging. He's brought the United States Government to its knees for want of gold."

A roaring wind turned the ambient smoke into a cyclone.

Stanislaw asked, "A sirocco?"

Bull drew his revolver. "Beamard's smelled out our gold!"

There came a lightning flash, then a steam explosion.

"My Puffy!"

Stanislaw ran for the locomotive, vanishing into the haze. Then he screamed, his cry whirling skyward. The cyclone became a tornado. Bull threw himself flat. The twister drew up all of the smoke, then reeled toward Superstition Peak.

Bull rose and searched his wrecked 4-4-0. He found the treasury chest gone. Bull weighed the few gold reales in his poke bag.

"I'll get you, Blazing Beamard!"

Across the desert, a pale town loomed. Bull started walking. The town receded as he advanced. Bull realized that it was a superior mirage: a trick of light bending over the horizon. He continued anyway, for the town *was* ahead, somewhere, and he saw no other refuge.

He broke out in clammy sweats. His temples throbbed. Bull cursed Beamard for stranding him. Suddenly, a cramp doubled him over. When he raised his head, his vision swam. Bull wondered where he was and fell prone.

...

Sulfurous water quenched his tongue. An Indian leaned above him. Bull reached for the man's water skin.

The Indian withdrew. "Take it easy." The Indian watered him slowly.

Bull croaked, "Where-you-from?"

"My home is nearby."

"In this hell-hole?"

"Living here wasn't our idea."

"Well, I'm glad. I thought I was a goner." Bull rose. "How far to the town?"

"Take my water."

...

Hours later, the foot-sore Special Agent reached a town called Nowhere. He limped along Main Street, past the horse trader and the general store, to the saloon.

The pianola within twanged out a dirge, while gloomy men drank. A scar-faced Sheriff watched four whores play poker. The winner, a Chinese girl, listlessly stuffed green-paper promissory notes down her cleavage.

Bull approached the bar.

"What suits your thirst, stranger?"

"Whiskey." He offered a gold bit-of-eight.

The sheriff snatched the *reale*. "Where'd you get this?"

"The mint."

The whores gathered around, wide-eyed. The Chinese girl licked her lips. She smiled at Bull, and opened her bodice. Green paper fluttered to the sawdust.

"Back off," the sheriff said, pushing her away.

Bull said, "Sheriff, I'm a Special Agent. I hereby deputize you and your men to help me apprehend the train robber known as Blazing Beamard."

The sheriff's brow darkened, and the men all looked fearful.

The whore giggled.

Bull asked, "What's funny?"

She replied, "Beamard's not a man!"

"What is he, then?"

"A dragon, not Dragon King or his Nine Sons, but a Western dragon, hungry for gold and human sacrifice."

Bull addressed the room. "I'll pay every man who aids me."

"I'll go," said the whore.

"Gold for every man!"

"I can handle a gun," said the whore.

The sheriff laughed. "You've handled every gun in town!"

Bull asked desperately, "Any man?"

All but the whore turned away.

"Then, I'm alone."

He went down Main Street to the horse trader. A few raw-boned animals milled in the paddock, munching withered grass.

The trader's eyes shifted. "All of my stock is sold."

"I've got gold."

The trader's eyes shone, but then he turned away. "All sold."

Bull went to the general store.

"I need provisions for the trail."

"I'm out of food."

"What's in those barrels?"

"Pig feed."

Bull showed his gold. The storekeeper turned away.

Bull limped out of town.

A masked highwayman confronted him. "Hands up!"

Bull recognized the man's build. "You've turned outlaw, sheriff?"

"You'll anger Beamard, just as this town's regaining a bit of peace. I'll give you one chance to return where you came from."

"I'm a lawman with a duty, you should understand that."

The sheriff sighed. "I do, and I'm sorry." He aimed between Bull's eyes.

The Chinese whore stepped from hiding, and shot the gun out of the sheriff's hand.

"Ouch! You've assaulted an officer of the law!"

"The United States Government will pardon her," said Bull. "I guess I do need your help, after all."

"My name is Fang." She whistled for two horses, both loaded with provisions. "Mount up, Bull."

"Where to?"

"Superstition Peak."

...

Blazing Beamard

The campfire banged in the night, startling their hobbled mounts.

"They know Beamard's near," said Fang.

"I don't believe in dragons."

"You saw the train wreck; how did a *man* do that?"

"Beamard's genius for invention is superseded only by his cold-hearted greed. I believe he's invented an air-borne pirate ship."

Fang laughed. "Your theory is ridiculous."

Her scoffing stung him. "Have you seen this dragon?"

"No, but I saw his vast shadow, heard his roar, and felt his breath. He razed Nowhere's bank, and flew away with the gold. The sheriff led a posse in chase—that's how he got his scars. Now, he appeases the dragon and notifies Beamard when the gold shipment is due, so the attack occurs far from town."

"With no gold, you trade that funny green paper?"

Fang pulled a note from her bodice. "Fiat money. Each bill represents a piece of Beamard's hoard." She tossed the bill into the fire. "How I crave gold!" Fang eyed Bull's poke.

He blushed. "I'm not that kind of a man."

"May I touch a reale? I promise I'll return it."

Bull relented.

Fang caressed her cheek with the gold, and moaned. "It feels so good!"

His blush heated. "You'd better give that back."

Fang popped the reale into her mouth and swallowed.

"That's government property!" Bull protested.

"Beamard won't have that nugget," Fang said smugly.

Bull opened his mouth for a crude retort, but then saw a huge, black shape rising from Superstition Peak. His flush drained cold.

"He's coming."

The thing rushed down at them. The horses screamed, and one stumbled attempting to flee.

Fang drew her gun. "All dragons have a weakness. We must find Beamard's!"

The dragon grew in perspective, blotting half the sky. Multiple wings propelled the thing, while a vertical tail steered. Dim, red eyes glowed above its snout.

"There!" Fang cried, and fired.

Bull joined her attack, the muzzle flashes lingering in his sights.

The dragon's wings raised a cyclone. Its jaws opened, and blue sparks jumped between its grillwork teeth, coalescing to form a thunderbolt. The lightning struck yards before its targets, but the concussion somersaulted Bull and Fang. Bull landed hard, limbs twitching and jerking against his will.

The dragon's lower jaw scraped the ground. With a steely rattle, a ship's anchor dropped, its flukes digging into the sand. The dragon swayed to a halt.

Bull regained control of his body, and stood, forlornly regarding his empty gun hand. No bones had broken, but he ached everywhere. He looked around.

"Fang?"

She did not reply.

Soldiers marched out of the dragon's iron jaws. Upon his breast, each man wore a badge with a yellow sun. They surrounded Bull, aiming their carbines.

Bull raised his hands. "I'm unarmed."

A large, bearish man descended the dragon's ramp. "I'm Beamard." He spoke with a rough Irish brogue. "You've interfered in my affairs."

"You've robbed my government to poverty."

"A necessity. I emigrated here to make my fortune, and save my starving homeland, but all that America offered me was brutal labor for small reward. With my Fenian brothers, I built this aerial galley, *Lig-na-Baste*, to take what I need. American gold will build a fleet of such vessels, and I will drive the British serpent from Ireland!"

The soldiers escorted Bull into the dragon's mouth. He looked back for Fang, wondering whether she had died in the lightning strike, or deserted him. The jaws ratcheted shut, their iron teeth interlocking. The anchor chain clanked onboard, and the galley teetered skyward. Bull grabbed a rail.

Beamard smirked. "You'll grow accustomed to it."

An overseer took charge of Bull, leading him down a narrow companionway to the galley deck. Dozens of men and women toiled there, shackled to handcar levers. Sweat stained their ragged clothing. The deck echoed with mechanical noise.

Bull said, "The people from the trains, and from Nowhere."

The overseer cuffed his ear, and indicated a lever where one man toiled alone.

"Smokey!"

"My. . . name's. . . Stanislaw!"

The overseer cuffed Bull again. "Adopt your chain!"

Bull cocked his fist but decided to wait, taking the lever opposite Stanislaw.

The overseer went to his station. A voice pipe whistled behind him, then Beamard's command barked from the cone:

"Starboard pumps feather!"

The overseer cried, "You heard the captain!"

The prisoners across the chamber altered their rhythm.

Bull leaned toward Stanislaw. "How does this thing work?"

"It's a giant. . . *Montgolfière* hot-air balloon. We're. . . powering. . . the wings. A huge gravity cell. . . collects atmospheric static. . . for the lightning gun."

"We must take this ship."

The overseer shouted, "Enough talk!"

Fang materialized behind the overseer. She struck him with the butt of her gun and stole the keys from the unconscious man.

"How did you get in here?"

"I slipped aboard while they arrested you." Fang snorted with contempt. "Foolish toy dragon!" She set about releasing Bull and Stanislaw and the other prisoners.

Beamard spoke through the pipe. *"Venting hydrogen. Pumps slow."* The ship angled down.

Bull said, "People, let's start this fight!" and pumped faster.

Beamard cried in panic, *"Slow down! Dump ballast!"*

Soldiers hurried into the galley deck, and grappled with the pumps.

The ship angled to rise, but the maneuver proved ineffective. The *Lig-na-Baste* struck earth belly-down, then bounced airborne, only to crash again. Soldiers and prisoners fell inter-tangled, like unsecured cargo in a storm-tossed ship. The *Lig-na-Baste* turned half over, and shuddered to an abrupt stop.

A soldier lurched to his feet, carbine waving at prisoners and comrades alike. Bull ended the man's confusion with a knockout punch and took up the carbine.

"People of Nowhere, revolt!"

Abandoning the resulting melee, Bull, Stanislaw, and Fang scrambled across the tilted deck to the ship's bridge, where Beamard dangled from the command throne's restraining harnesses.

Bull laughed and said, "You're under arrest!"

Beamard freed his harness's latch, and dropped onto Bull. The impact drove Bull to the canted deck, and crushed out his wind. Beamard wrested the carbine away, discarding the weapon to pummel Bull with fisticuffs.

Bull tried to block, but his enemy's strength turned his own forearms into bludgeons. Stars filled his eyes.

A pistol spoke. Beamard cried out, and rolled aside, fingers grasping his leg.

Fang's revolver smoked. "Show me the gold."

Bull recovered his feet, and his weapon. "You heard the lady."

"I can't walk!"

"Sure you can, that's just a flesh wound."

Stanislaw kicked Beamard, then jumped with a stubbed toe. "Move, you damn slaver!"

Beamard limped to his feet, and opened the dragon's mouth.

The ship lay on the mountain's plateau. Torches surrounded the landing area, and a few smoldered beneath *Lig-na-Batse's* fabric skin. Men feverishly stamped out the embers. Bunkhouses and a manse stood around the landing field. Irish carbines greeted Bull.

"Tell your men to stand down," he ordered.

Beamard looked truculent. Fang put her gun to his head, and thumbed the hammer.

Beamard gritted his teeth. "Do as he said."

The soldiers lowered their arms.

Stanislaw slapped Beamard's back, and chortled. "Lead on, Macduff!"

Beamard growled, replying, "The line is, 'Lay on'!" but led them inside the manse, and to an iron vault.

Fang panted. "Open it."

Beamard hesitated. "Please, thousands of my kin have starved! This gold is my only chance of repelling the British, and saving the rest—"

"Open it!"

Beamard worked the lock. The tumblers shifted heavily. Beamard opened the squealing door. Raw gold nuggets tumbled out. Sacks of coins lay within, and bags of gold dust, and piled ingots.

Fang snatched a nugget, and stuffed it into her mouth. She gagged for a moment, then swallowed hard. Fang next grabbed a poke bag of dust, and pursed her lips around its opening.

Bull yanked the bag away. "Are you loco, woman?"

Gold dust clung down her chin. Her green-blazing eyes fixed on Bull, and he backed away.

"I am descended of dragons, you ignorant primitive!"

Fang seized an ingot. Her fingers grew hooked claws, scoring the precious metal. Her jaws unhinged to receive the gold bar. Fang moaned ecstatically as the ingot slid down her throat.

Her skin cracked in a diamond-back pattern.

"She's not human," said Stanislaw, retreating.

Fang expanded. Her clothing split and fell away, revealing her new, serpentine physique. Antlers sprouted behind her ears. Membranous wings developed from her ribs. Fang gobbled Beamard's hoard, her spiked tail lashing. Fang's coils filled the vault room.

I thought she said only the western dragons were hungry for gold, Bull thought.

Bull and Stanislaw fired. Their bullets ricocheted from her gilded scales. Fang turned her cat-like eyes upon them, and hissed. The three men fled. The dragon pursued them, bursting the doorway, then snaking through the hall.

Beamard staggered behind Bull and Stanislaw on his injured leg. Suddenly, he shrieked. Bull glanced back at the muffled cry, and saw Beamard's feet kicking from the dragon's throat.

Bull and Stanislaw halted on the veranda. Irish soldiers waited outside.

Fang hit the exit, but the masonry wall stopped her. She groped with her prehensile, forked tongue and snatched Bull. The soldiers shifted their aim to the dragon, and fired. Fang released Bull, and yawned through the doorway. Her throat expelled a ball of fire into the soldiers' formation. The men scattered, trailing smoke and screaming, ammunition bursting in their red-hot carbines.

Bull and Stanislaw bolted down the veranda, then across the yard to the landing field.

With an enraged howl, Fang rammed her way out of the manse, and gave chase, floating like thistledown on a dozen laterally paired wings. Her tiny, clawed feet gouged the earth.

Stanislaw said, "This is one hell of a fix!"

"Can you drive that airship, Smokey?"

"My name's—oh, forget it! Sure I can, if she's not busted."

Beamard's overseer waited in the bridge, horse pistols in each hand. "Back to your chains, Yankees!"

Impact rocked the *Lig-na-Baste*. Fang's head rammed up the ramp. The overseer screamed, and turned his weapons upon the monster, without effect. He lowered his smoking barrels, and stood trembling.

Stanislaw crawled over the ship's control board. "Ah ha!" He yanked a lever.

Gears clicked. The ramp lifted, catching Fang's head. She struggled for a moment, then withdrew.

Stanislaw cried, "Where's the blam-jam ballast dump?"

The overseer pointed.

Stanislaw yanked another lever. There came a waterfall sound, and the ship lurched upward.

Stanislaw thrust his mouth to the voice pipe. *"Folks? I know you've been poorly used, but if you could work those pumps a little longer, I'd sure appreciate it."*

The overseer said, "I'll encourage them," and ran aft.

Bull looked out through a porthole, squinting against the dawn's light. Fang rose in pursuit, flying as a snake swims. Her wings cracked like thunder.

"Smokey, turn us around so I can shoot her."

Stanislaw peered at a dial, then shook his head. "The lightning gun needs more charge."

Fang released her flames. The attack fell short, but. . .

"She'll burn us out of the sky before it's ready!" Bull remembered what Fang herself had said: *All dragons have a weakness.*"—And I know hers!"

He opened the porthole, and dropped out his poke bag.

Fang's eyes flashed. She veered after the plummeting bag, and snapped up the gold. She brushed the earth, then pulled a hard loop back into the sky. At the top of her arc she rolled, and charged the *Lig-na-Baste* head on.

Stanislaw crowed, "We're loaded!"

The ship opened its jaws.

Fang replied in kind.

Sparks flew between the ship's teeth, massing forward.

Incandescence whirled in Fang's throat, then erupted.

Lightning hurtled from the ship's jaws.

Both shots struck home.

The *Lig-na-Baste's* bow exploded in flames, which rushed back to engulf the whole ship. Her skin burned off, leaving a delicate, glowing framework, twisting down toward earth.

Fang swelled and detonated.

. . .

A Hopi man named Cheauka looked up, startled by thunder from the clear sky. Cheauka had saved Bull's life in the desert, although Bull had never asked his nation or his name. Cheauka watched the *Lig-na-Baste's* fiery lattice flutter down, a half-mile away.

Something wet struck Cheauka's face. He wiped the spot, then shuddered at the blood on his hand.

A heavy object plummeted at his feet. Cheauka jumped back, then stared in wonder at the golden ingot which had dropped from the sky.

###

About the Author

Stanley Webb resides on a tiny homestead in upstate New York, near the coastline of Lake Ontario.

Throughout his life, he has worked as a dishwasher, a cook, a video rental clerk, and in the automobile industry. He now lives in early retirement.

Stanley's parents weaned him on *Monster Movie Matinee*. When he attended elementary school, his teachers would have preferred a greater interest in lessons, and less interest in sketching dinosaurs.

Stanley discovered storytelling during kindergarten's mandatory nap sessions. Eventually, he learned to record and polish his tales, and marketed the stories through the United States Postal Service.

Years passed, and his writing skills matured. His work has now found many homes, including the anthologies *Jack Lanterns, Death and Decorations*, and an incipient issue of *Weirdbook Magazine.*

Stanley thanks all who have read his stories.

*****~~~~~*****

Lampblack and Dust

by J. L. Forrest

The Ice-Dusters snatched my brother and niece, dragged them into the Dust after a nighttime raid which left thirteen missing and thirty-one dead. Always been my brother's big sister, yes, but this time I weren't nowhere nearby to help. Didn't know nothing about it till nightfall, when I seen the fires glow as I came down from the Ponderosas. I throttled fast as I could for the flats, riding so quick I was afraid I'd blow the pistons from my machine. A quarter of New Water burned, and I was too late by a horizon.

My rage told me to hurry after the Dusters, to conjure fiercely and unholster my ironpieces. Though now, drowning my heartache in the Ricka Saloon, I spin ink into my whiskey, and the swirls tell me to nurture my patience. They tell me I'll need diversions, and they tell me such diversions are coming.

The Marshals seldom travel out so far as New Water, but this time they do on account of so many being murdered, on account of our sheriff lying dead, on account of a Duster's remains now sitting in our mortuary. We buried our own but, though it stinks something awful, we leave the Duster for the lawmen.

"By the gods," says the High Marshal, holding his nose above the cadaver, "I ain't never seen anything like this."

"Who killed it?" another Marshal asks.

"Father Patrick," says the undertaker.

"Might we speak with him?"

"No, sir. We buried him yesterday."

The Marshals frown at each other. The townies *did* put up a fight, slung heaps of lead, but stories abound of Dusters shrugging off bullets like mosquitoes. Only the Father's ironpiece, an old pistol like my pair, found its mark.

Some say Dusters ain't human or maybe they once was but ain't no more. But this much I know—my brother and his daughter, out there in the Dust, they *ain't* dead. They're still kicking, waiting on some suffering, because I seen what Ice-Dusters do to those they capture, those they Tap. It ain't pretty.

So I tell High Marshal McIntyre I want to ride beside him. That with my help, he and his men might survive.

"There ain't nothing," he says to me, hoping to cool my fire, my hankering to follow Jak and rescue his little girl, "out in the Dust for an Orioness to do." McIntrye gives me the eye—the grizzled coot, his sense of justice like granite, his sympathies like warmed-over haggis. "Best you stay in New Water, Ms. Hauston. You wait, and we'll come back with your family."

The ink also told me this—every newfound Orioness reaches the Ponderosas of Lampblack only after deep personal loss, only after something awful done happened. Seems this time it'll unfold no different.

"You won't," I say.

McIntrye hawks his chaw. "Why so cocksure?"

"The ink, it told me."

Of the Marshals, only McIntyre looks me in the eye. My ink often unsettles decent folk, even lawmen, slithering cross my skin like it does, and some people say my eyes are right frightening. The townies only gawk when I ain't looking back, only whisper when they think I ain't listening. That's how it is, being what I am, but I abide because of my brother, because he took a townie wife, because sweet Maybell gave him my niece and nephew.

"The ink?" McIntyre laughs, as if dismissing a niggling fear. "We don't need no witch's parlor tricks. Stay in town, woman. Couple of days, we'll be back with *all* who the Ice-Dusters done stole."

The High Marshal spoke sideways, of course—there's plenty out in the Dust for me to do, now my brother and sweet niece are in it, and the Marshals could use an Orioness's good turn—but what he's really opining is this: *We don't want no pythoness around. We don't like you. Nobody does.*

It ain't against the law no more, being an Orioness, not since the Pope done forgave us. Now and then, though, the law sure finds excuses to lynch us—during the daytime, of course—and I ain't going to try too hard to convince the Marshals of their folly. Who knows, mayhap the High Marshal's right, and it's the ink which tells me wrong. Such things *can* happen, men being correct when the spirits ain't.

I acquiesce and let the Marshals go.

At dawn of the fourth day, with my sister-in-law and nephew cold in the ground, these Marshals fuel up their machines, load their guns, and blaze southward into the Dust. They head for the Canyons, beyond the horizon, for what they call the *extrajudicial territories.*

In a few hours I will follow, but not till after dark. Nightfall business awaits me.

...

The graveyard spreads north from town, where the expanding salts haven't yet infected the savanna. As the quarter moon passes zenith, a stale wind rises, and I trudge past thirty new plots nestled amongst the hundreds of older markers. The scent of fresh-turned earth guides me, and I kneel at the graves of Maybell and her little boy, Greene. As I press my hand to the still-soft dirt, it tickles my palm, and I caress the broken clay as I might have caressed Greene's cheek. For a spell, all I can do is sob out my love for that boy.

I will *not* summon him—it'd be a step too cruel—so instead I lie across my sister-in-law's ground. I'd embrace her if I could, but that time is passed.

After dark, my ink drinks the lightlessness, gains strength, and vivifies. I breathe glyphs over the ground which holds what was Maybell, trilling as the symbols slide from my face and throat and hands. From my flesh the indelible illustrations flow, whorls seething with meaning and which quiver through all creation. The inks swim forth to gambol upon the grave.

And Maybell rises.

She sits, confused and gaunt, beneath the panoply of stars, then shrieks and claws and shakes. But Maybell is a shade and so can harm no one. I take her face in my hands, insubstantial as it is, and caress her cheeks to calm her.

"Tell me, sister," I say to her, "tell me all from the moments before you died. Tell me everything, anything which might help me save your husband and little Parilla."

"I seen the Dusters," she says. "I seen one's eyes, like a gila."

"Did you witness as to the one Father Patrick killed?"

"Bullets twice blest." She nods. "Once over the bullet box, once before he fired."

Do the blessings of an Orioness match those of a Father? Hell if I got a clue, but I know for a fact the *padre* was a lousy shot.

"How many Ice-Dusters were there?" I ask.

"Fourteen, and a swarm of bullets we wasted on them." She offers me a sorrowful simper, as if I might be joining her soon. "Bring your old ironpieces," she tells me, then she uses my name, "Faireweather, bring your ironpieces and plenty of lead. Plenty! And bless it twice!"

"Bullets I can bless," I say, lifting my chin. "Bullets I can sling."

"What else can one do, sister?" She moans with the pain of holding too long to the wrong realm.

"Thank you, Maybell. Rest well and sweetly."

Maybell fades into oblivion.

...

An hour later, I straddle my machine, my ironpieces in their holsters, wearing two bandoliers with bullets already once blest. I speed south, the machine's chassis humming between my knees, its repellers thrumming. Years ago, men and women rode horses, but few of those remain, like so many other beasts fallen to Rot. Technology replaced animal labor, first the great clockworks of masters like Von Zerstörer. Then the steam phenomenon of Watts. Now the science-magic of Curie, whose discoveries power *my* machine. I lower my visor, open the throttle, and the velocitometer hits 120. Behind me, the moonlight silvers across a wan cloud of salt.

I look over my shoulder, mayhap one last time at New Water. Lightless splotches reveal where the Ice-Dusters torched the church and a dozen houses, but the rest of New Water's sodium lights flicker somberly over the dry plains. I note the bright lamps of the Ricka, where Toothless Jarith has so often poured my ryes, where the upstairs girls are some of the few who don't recoil from me, where there's always a warm bed.

Mayhap I *won't* be back. Mayhap that's alright. Soon I'll go up to the Ponderosas again, where it'll be a new time for teaching and learning, like as when I was a little girl.

Settlers weren't meant for this flat-pan desert anyhow, not meant for silt and salt, all their imported wood now leaning and bleached and bowed. Kind of like its residents, all losing a slow battle against the Dust, which grows by yards every year. What in the hells do I care about the townies now?

I throttle to 140 and go all out till dusk the next night.

. . .

Silt crusts each iota of my body, and, after a night and day of riding, I'm dirtier than any sin. Long past sunset, I belly crawl to the edge of a bluff, overlooking the Canyons. Hellfire brews down there, where the Ice-Dusters' contraptions belch soot above the furnace-shine and smelting-glow of their foundries. The enormity of their operation gives me pause. A dozen stupendous steel apparatuses chew the canyon sides, and hundreds of the Tapped labor in the rubble, thralls to the Dusters.

Bedlam. All to extract Ice.

People in the cities, they pay odious prices for it. For them, a drug.

For the Tapped, it's a stay of execution. Too long a spell without it brings death.

Though overseers, the Dusters don't carry no weapons, not so much as pistols, as they don't fear no uprisings. They don't wear no armor neither, only wrap themselves in linens head to toe like 'gyptian mummies, though even during the night they goggle their eyes.

I breathe hoodoo through my ink, and a brace of ravens flutters from the lineaments of my shoulders, wisping along on wings of black gauss. As they fly I borrow their vision, gandering round the mine entrances, over the fiery contrivances, past the rows of glassy-eyed Tapped, even swooping close enough to spy the slender steel tubes protruding from the bases of their skulls, *tapping* their spines. The Tapped.

Three Marshals ain't nothing but meat now, flayed on crosses. Turning from them, my corvid eyes study the vista, and darn near fifty more bodies cram a nearby trench, probably all the poor Tapped who the Marshals had to gun down before the masses overwhelmed them. I imagine the lawmen's confusion, having to lead-belly people they thought they was coming to save.

I tried to tell High Marshal McIntyre this was going to happen. I seen it, swirling my inks in Toothless Jarith's whiskey shots. Divination, they call it, and the spirits seldom lie.

Two Marshals ain't yet dead, and the Dusters crowd around them in some godsforsaken ceremony, prodding and having their sport as the lawmen scream. Maybe those men will live on, as Tapped, but probably not. I reckon tonight they're crossing into the Dark, and being lawmen and not magi, they ain't coming back. Ain't much doing for them now, so I wing past them into a side canyon guarded by three somber Tapped.

My heart leaps!

Ain't no sign of Jak, but in the back of a cage my sweet Parilla cringes, hugging her knees, her sable curls matted across her forehead. Tears streak her face. I alight one raven upon the cage's bars, while my second bird overflies the sulfurous infernos around the Ice mines. It finds the Marshals' machines, set aside for slagging, clustered nearer the foundries.

In a cage beside my niece's, McIntyre grips the bars and glowers into the dark. Though stripped of guns, beaten and bloodied, his eyes remain clear, still searching for his granite justice. Mayhap he'd find it, if only he could escape his steel cage.

Beyond McIntyre's prison are six more, all holding hungry, thirsty, disheartened figures.

Thirty yards downhill, an Ice-Duster approaches the guardsmen. In turn, each man supplicates hisself and exposes the back of his neck. The Duster unstoppers the taps, leaches the men's fluids, and pours into those cavities a powdering of Ice. After the mummy departs, the men stand and wobble, dazed by the drug rush, given another stretch of existence.

"Sarsaparilla!" I whisper, through my raven, to my niece.

The girl blinks and, being the smarty she is, she says, "Auntie Faireweather?"

"Your cage will open, precious girl. You will leave it and hide nearby till I arrive. Understood?"

She nods.

"Where's you father?" I ask.

"They took him."

The ink told me they would. In the timeline where I traveled with the Marshals, Jak lives. In this one, he don't, and there ain't no changing it.

McIntyre gapes, staring too at the blurry, slippery form of my raven. "Sakes alive! All the stories *are* true—"

"Not *all*," I snap back, "or the Pope would still be burning us."

"My apologies, ma'am."

"Your cage will open too, Marshal, and you've time to act, but not much—the Dusters are still occupied, piling the hurt on your remaining friends."

Clenching his jaw, McIntyre nods.

"Question is," I say, my words clicking through a bird's throat, "you with me?"

"My men—Carstelle and Timmel—what chance they got?"

"Slim to none."

He sets his jaw, gesturing toward the other prisoners. "Then let's get these good folks out of here."

"Leave my niece behind, Marshal, but the rest are yours."

I tell him where the Marshals' machines are parked, how the escapees can reach them. Then my raven ceases to exist, bursting into feathers and airy wisps of jet that pour into the cages' locks. A wraithy whisper hums through the metal, a clang follows, and all the prisoners go free.

...

Some of my conjurations possess ample brawn to heft a ten-year-old girl. Some can shimmy up cliffs. None can manage both, so I drop rope and rappel. I've a half-mile to cover, and quick, so I jog it. My boots ain't for sprinting, but still I hurry through the lung-scorching vapors of the slag fields. I pass the clangor of the apparatuses and the vacuous-eyed rows of the Tapped, who focus only on their labors. For now they pay me no mind, but at a Duster's command, they'd bum-rush me like a tide of angry meat, piles too many to ever shoot or ensorcel.

Yet for now I'm safe. Near the junction where Parilla holes up, the Dusters still epicurate over Carstelle's and Timmel's torture.

Slinking through the side canyon, seeking my niece, I mutter life into the inks along my belly. A flutter of bats squeak into the dark, and they assure me there ain't no surprises awaiting. Ain't no sign of McIntyre or the others, neither, who're by now almost to the machines. They'll break for it soon, try their escape.

I need them to, need the roar of their engines, the Dusters screaming after them, the dullard mob of Tapped thralls rushing to overwhelm the riders. *Diversions.* I can't say for sure who'll live or die—the inks ain't so unequivocal—but not all of McIntyre's will make it.

That I *do* know.

Weren't never meant to, and here's the truth—I care about only one, and right now her small hand grasps mine.

At last, McIntyre revs his engines and the townies follow him. The Dusters shriek in surprise and, while they run past us, I crouch with my arms around Parilla. We keep low, out of sight, and stay there as hundreds of

Tapped chase the escaped townies and the High Marshal, scampering past us far too quickly for humans, heedless of their own bodies' limitations. I never reckoned on so many! The mines vomit them, or they scuttle from the apparatuses, so many as to constitute an army. They pour by, but soon the pour becomes a trickle, and the trickle becomes none.

"Come on," I say to Parilla. I conjure a panther to carry her, and we hurry the other way, back to the rope I left for our ascent.

A rope no longer there.

An Ice-Duster awaits us with a score of Tapped. Our battle is short and brutal, their side all zombie strength and careless determination, my side a menagerie of fangs and talons alongside a double blaze of ironpieces and slinging lead.

"Twice blest," I pray, and the fracas ends only when my bullet splits the Duster's goggles, leaving the mummy belly up, dead-gecko eyes fixed skyward.

I do not point out to Parilla that her daddy lies among the expired.

Instead, I crouch and carry her piggyback. "Come on, sweetie, hold on tight."

Some witches fly, but I ain't one. I restore my inks to my skin, climb the stark cliff with a ten-year-old weighing me down, and at the top it's a spell before I do anything but lie there and pant. Long before dawn, though, I ride north with Parilla on the seat cowl, her arms around my middle.

"Auntie Faireweather?" she asks, yelling over the motor's growl.

"Yes, sweetie?"

"We going to New Water?"

She don't understand yet about her parents, about her brother. I ain't up for telling her quite yet.

"No, honey," I say, "we're going way north, take something of a holiday, visit the Coven in the Ponderosas of Lampblack."

"What happens there, auntie?"

I cannot decide whether to cry or laugh. "Why, there they train the Orionesses. It's where a girl gets her first ink. It's where I got mine."

###

About the Author

J. L. Forrest scrawls from the frosty mountains of Colorado, from the Old Country of Roma, Italia, and from the wet techno-wilds of the Pacific Northwest. He is an active member of the Science Fiction and Fantasy Writers of America, and his stories have appeared in numerous publications. Reach him at http://jlforrest.com or on Twitter @WordForrest.

*****~~~~~*****

The Quiet Crime

by Jordan Ashley Moore

On a late Saturday afternoon the light fell across the top of the dresser, across the two guns that lay there, the weapons Sam Stein had carried for over forty years. He had been a law enforcement officer, once. He had been a sheriff. Now his hair was running white, and he was stooped, and old. He looked at the two weapons for a long time, not moving. Finally he held them up and holstered them, one at his side, one against his leg, and went out to his truck. It was a gray day, a warm day, and he drove along the Texas highways with his arm hanging out the window, across the river and into the back roads of Presidio County.

He rode thirty miles, along the highways and down old dirt drives, out to the western part of the county, where the homes were falling down and the old barns and tool sheds were standing in their places like memorials. The sun beat down as the sweat gathered at his temples, and he looked out with his watery eyes into the Texas countryside.

He saw the home in the distance, as the sun went down, and he slowed the truck and pulled up to the drive. Lighting a cigarette he sat in the driveway and looked at it, the old wood home with the tin roof. There was empty country beside it, and nothing else. The wind was blowing, and the dust along with it. Finally he stepped out of the truck, put out his cigarette in the white dust, and knocked three times on the oak door.

He stood there a long time, as the wind caught up around him, and he could barely make out the sounds inside, the footsteps on the old hardwood.

"This is Sam Stein," he said, in his hoarse voice. "I was just out this way, figured I'd stop in. I can come later if you're busy."

The door opened, and John Mercer leaned out, older than he had been the last time, older than he should have been. He nodded to the sheriff and looked out, his eyebrows knotted above his drooping nose, his eyes wild, his mouth opened slightly as if it couldn't shut.

"Sheriff?" he said. "Is that you?"

"It is," Sam told him. The old man held onto the door and looked out at him like he was waiting for him to say something else. There was a gun in his hand, behind the door, and Sam was aware that there was.

"What you doing all the way out here?" he said. "Am I in some kind of trouble or something?"

Sam shook his head, and touched his hat. "Ain't no trouble. I just wanted to stop by and see you. I figure we're not either of us getting any younger. You mind if I come in?"

John looked back at him and bent his head a little, as if considering. "Come on in," he said, finally. "Place doesn't look like much."

Sam took off his hat and entered, placing his boots down on the hard floor and breathing in the scent of the home, the old leather furniture and the dusty fireplace. John shut the door behind him and waited for him to take a seat at the old pinewood table by the window, where the last of the light was coming in. It was evening, now, and the horizon was a white place, almost no place at all, and Sam sat in the white light as John strained toward the table, struggling with his good leg and trying to hide it at the same time.

"Well, how've you been getting along?" Sam asked him, propping his legs up. The older man sat at the table across from him and leaned against the wall, just out of the light, and looked across at him with his tanned skin and his hands like the veins of a dried riverbed.

"About like hell," he said, shaking his head slightly. "Getting worse every day. This leg's been giving me fits. Can't sleep at night, neither. Yeah, I'd say I haven't been doing worth a damn. So how about you? You still doing the sheriff thing?"

Sam shook his head and looked out the window, out into the distance.

"I still got my health," he said, in his deep voice, drawling the words with care and leaning back in his seat. "They run me out years ago, from being sheriff. I'm surprised you hadn't heard about it. Said I was just being too hard. They had reporters from all over the country coming and talking to me. Sons of bitches are real brave when they're behind a camera."

The house creaked in the wind, and John still looked ahead at him. "Well I'm sorry to hear that," he said. "Things is definitely changed from when you and I was growing up." Sam nodded, looking down at the table, and John watched him. "So, what's wrong?" he asked. "I can tell something's wrong. You didn't just come by here for nothing."

"It's nothing," Sam said, putting his hands on the table with a sigh. They were large, rough hands, like his father's. "Just been thinking about old things, things that never got solved, put away to my satisfaction."

John didn't move, as he looked at him. He just stared across, in the dark. "You thinking of anything in particular?"

Sam nodded his head, and settled forward in his seat, leaning his elbows down on the table so that the holster was briefly exposed at his side.

"You remember that old boy that came through here from the border years back, name of Rodriguez? One that killed those two sheriff's deputies, not a mile or two from out here?"

John nodded his head, and lowered his eyes. "I remember," he said. "I can't hardly forget."

"I been thinking about that," Sam said. "Came through that night, and killed some men, and went off in the hills, and was never seen again. We called a manhunt, I was new then, and I went out in them hills myself. Tracks all around this place. It seems like he never left. But he did. Somehow he did. Like he just lifted off the ground."

"I remember it," John said, his eyes empty as night. "It worried my wife about to death. She was never the same from that day on. Didn't feel safe around the house. She started getting where she couldn't sleep at night. I lost a few nights of sleep, myself, after that day, I won't lie. I never could figure it. I just stopped worrying about it."

"I never did," Sam said, nodding slowly. "I been thinking about it all this time. Twenty, thirty years ago, now, that it happened, and still been keeping me up at night. Just that he got away. That he has to be out there, somewhere. And you don't know where. I been thinking, and thinking, until it just about come to me, one at a time, just slow."

John looked up at him through his eyebrows. "Well, what?" he said. "What are you saying? I don't follow you."

Sam looked around, in the dark. There was an old stove sitting up on a board, not far from him, with its grill open and part of its front blackened. In the living room there was a stone fireplace with one of the pokers missing.

In the back of the room across from the window there was a gun rack with dark oak panels. He only saw it because the light fell on it. One of the racks was empty; the case had been opened, and the right door hung out.

"I been trying to figure it," Sam said. "Fellow shot two men, walked into a canyon, out in the hills, and he's never seen or heard from again. It's like he came here, he came into this place, and he never left it. So I got to thinking, maybe he never did leave."

John knotted his brows and stared at him. "Like he died? You saying he went out there and died? They searched that whole mountain range, Sam. Did it more than once. There wasn't no man out there."

"No, no man at all," Sam said, quietly, leaning back. John just looked at him, with his mouth partly open, like he was trying to understand.

"Then what the hell are you saying?"

"You been following the news?" John shook his head. "Well. There's been all kind of things going on. Things you wouldn't even believe. People disappearing, and reappearing, and everything just going to shit. Real quiet, you know, like it isn't anything. Like all these people that just disappear around here, across the border, and turn up with their heads cut off. It's like that. Except it isn't that, it isn't that at all. It isn't gangs, it isn't Mexicans."

"Well, what is it?" John asked.

Sam breathed in heavily, and put up his hands again. "We had a boy go missing down in Marfa," he said, in a quiet voice. "Name of Jim Baker, never hurt anyone, never bothered no one. I knew him by my brother-in-law, met him one time. He went missing years back, came back with a different car, talking strange, acting funny. His wife thought he was having a nervous breakdown or something. This was in 2003, when I was still on the force. He lived for years like that, couldn't keep a job, went on unemployment. They thought he had lost his mind. Well, they found him by the side of the road over in Jeff Davis County about three years ago. His head was all torn up, like he'd been shot, or run over, or something. Just a hell of a thing."

John nodded his head. "So, what happened to him?"

Sam looked him in his eyes. The light was starting to go down, and he could barely see him, now, in the dark. His hands were placed carefully below the table, where he couldn't see them.

"They did a autopsy," he said. "Couldn't find anything out of the ordinary. Just the shots, and the bones broken up and all that. They were going to give him over to the family. They come in the next morning to take him out, and the body was all black. Like the skin had fallen out, just fallen away, and the bones was different. Now I never seen any of this myself. This was over in Lobo. I just heard about it later. They had a man there said he thought God had reached down and changed the world, like he had walked in on a thing out of Scripture. They tried to get a team in there, to see, but it was falling all to pieces. By the time they got there it was all gone. It just come apart on the floor. And it wasn't a man, in the end, whatever it was. It was just a thing, pretending to be a man."

The wind shook the house again, and the first slow rolls of thunder far off in the distance. John licked his lips, across from him, and folded his hands like he was waiting for him to say something with some actual sense. Sam cleared his throat, and spoke up again.

"I don't know what it is," he said. "I don't know what it means. All I know is there was a man grew up around here, nicest man you could meet, and one day he woke up and he wasn't a man. Like something had taken him over. Some folks are saying the end times are here. You read about those things coming down and hurting people in Revelation. Horrible things. Things that shouldn't ever be seen on this earth. I used to think it was all just a story, you know. Just to scare people. And now they got things from some other place, coming and taking what we have. Till you can't hardly tell the difference. They could be living right next door to you. They could be talking to you on the phone, or in your home. And you wouldn't know."

John looked out the window like he was expecting to see something. Like something might lean out of the wilderness and explain things to him, or make it clear to him.

"I don't understand," he said, his voice shrill. "I'm an old man. You come out here all this way just to tell me this? About aliens or something? What the hell does this have to do with anything?"

Sam looked him in the eye, and licked his lips. His hands were on the table, and they were white, pressed down against the smooth wood.

"That man came through here not a mile from this house, twenty years ago," he said. "Shot up two men, left them laying, and he went off. I mean he could be anywhere, you see. He could be anyone. But I just got to thinking, why would he be? It would be the easiest thing in the world to stay right here. Never even leave the crime scene, so to speak. He'd just have to find someplace nice. Some place out of the way."

The house settled, and John put his hand down at his side. Sam could just see the stock of the gun from where he was sitting, the long rifle on the bench beside him.

"Now, what exactly are you saying?" John asked him. His hand was shaking, and his eyes were dilated. "You trying to say something happened here?"

Sam sat still, and looked across at him. There was a sheen on his face, the man across from him, barely visible in the light, and a look in his eye, like he was thinking about something, wrestling with something. Almost like he was holding it in the air.

"I know something happened," he said, after a while. "I just don't know what it was. I looked in that man's eyes, a mile from this house, and he looked back at me. Looked like any Mexican you ever seen. But I know he wasn't. There was something in those eyes. Something that wasn't from around these parts. It was like a wild animal was looking back at me. A wounded animal. He was afraid, John. He was trying to find a place to hide. You know what I'm saying?"

John's hands on the table were curled up like he was about to stand. His eyes were set in his head, as he looked at Sam, and Sam couldn't make them out. They were just looking. Like there wasn't anyone inside looking at all.

"I never did like this country," Sam said, slowly. "Ever since I was a boy. I was afraid to come out here, when I was young. I could never say why. Just felt out of the way, I guess. I been getting a cold feeling in my gut every time I come out to these parts, and walk these hills. I've been doing it for twenty years. Like there's something here that don't belong. You understand what I'm saying?"

John looked at him and nodded slowly, turning to look at the window. Sam could see the side of his face, old, carved like stone, and the last bit of light fell on it.

"I been seeing things," he said. "Lights, out in the desert. Things moving around, crawling, just moving. Like things I ain't ever seen before. I was thinking it was just my mind. I been real lonely out here, since my wife died. Sometimes I wonder if I had just passed away, in the night, and no one ever told me. Like nothing's really even out here at all."

Sam looked at his hat, beside him, and nodded. "I heard you wasn't doing so good," he said. "Heard they took you in one day up at the store, because you got lost.

You took it hard, didn't you, when your wife died? Really shook you up."

John nodded his head, his mouth open, as if he was in a stupor. He turned to Sam, and Sam stood as if to leave.

"So what is this really about?" John asked, in a quiet voice. "Why'd you come all the way out here, to see an old man?"

"I just wanted to see you," Sam said, as carefully as he could. "Talk to you a little. See if you had changed any. You know. How old people do. Just wanted to let you know I was watching out for you. I don't want you to get too lonely out here."

John looked down at the floor and stood a moment. He made his way to the door, and opened it. The wind was playing against it, and it came in all of a sudden, the sound of it. Sam held on to his hat and walked up to the door, and nodded to John. It was starting to rain, just lightly, a nice, quiet patter on the dry ground and dust.

"It was like this that day out on the range," Sam said, looking out. "That day my Daddy brought over those gas cans, and we put them in the shed. He was still driving that old rusty '38 Ford. You remember that?"

John looked out, too, and pursed his lips. "I can't rightly say," he said, his eyes drifting. "I don't remember much these days."

Sam gazed into the distance, his right hand firmly against the gun at his side. The wind cried, and the thunder, and all the world was a shadow. He looked at that countryside, at its wilderness and its darkness, and he turned back and looked at John, at the old man in the frame of his house, broken down and at the end of his life. "I guess some things can't be helped," he said. "I'll see you. One way or the other."

He walked out into the rain, and opened his truck. John watched him start the truck, and he watched him back out into the wet Texas road, turning and easing out into the distance. He stood as if in a dream, looking out on a strange landscape where unfamiliar things moved in the distance. And Sam looking back at him saw only a lost thing, a phantom who might only dimly remember that truck, on a warm summer day, in the evening, with the clouds coming, as he turned back into his house, into the dark, and shut the door.

###

About the Author

Jordan Ashley Moore lives in Walker, Louisiana, with a growing collection of wild animals that includes four cats and two voracious miniature dachshunds. His short stories have appeared previously in *Origins: Colliding Causalities* and *Abbreviated Epics*, both by Third Flatiron, and his poetry has appeared in *Blue Unicorn*. He also reads whimsical ancient literature on YouTube as the Ancient Literature Dude.

*****~~~~~*****

The Monster Hunter

by Angus McIntyre

Whitmore Braddock, celebrated hunter of monsters and lesser beasts, made his entry into Litton's Hollow with characteristic bravado. Leaping down from the stage before the wheels had fully stopped turning, he crossed the street in six long strides and threw open the swinging doors of the saloon with the force of a tornado.

I looked up from a glass I was drying and saw him silhouetted in the doorway, peering into the gloom as if to assure himself that the daytime drinkers around the bar constituted an audience big enough to be worthy of his presence. Apparently satisfied, he swung the leather grip off his shoulder and let it fall to the weathered floorboards with a crash like a pair of locomotives falling down a mountain.

"Men," he roared. "I'm Whitmore Julius Braddock." He paused. "And I can outdrink, outfight, and outscrew any sonofabitch in this sorry excuse for a town."

The people of my hometown are not much versed in philosophy, but they have certain empirical leanings. Extraordinary claims require extraordinary proof. We had heard of Braddock, of course—who hadn't?—but some things you don't just take on faith.

Over the next few hours, he demonstrated the proof of his first claim so convincingly that no one felt the need to challenge him on the other two.

"Whisky!" Braddock boomed, surging up to the bar like a tidal wave. I made to pour him a shot, but he plucked the bottle out of my hand, pulled the cork with his teeth, spat it neatly over the piano, and drank a slug straight from the bottle. He blinked twice, and then his eyes focused on me.

"Boy!" he growled (an easy mistake to make; in those days I kept my hair short and wore men's clothes most of the time). He jerked a thumb over his shoulder. "Take my bag up to my room." Then he stuck the bottle back in his mouth and tipped his head back for another swig.

The bag weighed almost as much as I did. After I somehow wrestled it up the stairs and dragged it down the corridor to the front guest-room, I gave in to the temptation to peek inside and find out what made it so damned heavy. Instead of pants and shirts, Braddock had filled his bag with enough weaponry to storm Mexico: machetes, knuckledusters, a brace of huge revolvers, a case of skinning knives, two scatterguns, and three feet of chain you could have used to tie up a steamboat. There was also a hip flask, four boxes of ammunition in different calibers, and a railway timetable as thick as a Bible.

By the time I returned to the saloon, the first bottle was a hollow ghost on the bar in front of Braddock, and he had started on a second. He was sipping more cautiously now, and his eyes were a little glazed—"Doc" Benson's white lightning commands respect even from monster hunters—but it was clear that the second bottle would soon follow the first.

Having taken the edge off his thirst and assured himself of an audience, Braddock swiveled on his stool, planted his elbows comfortably on the bar, and surveyed the room. He gestured for me to pour for anyone who wanted it, then lifted his bottle in salute.

"Lads," he said. "Now you're all listening, I'm going to give you a little lecture on my favorite subject." His face split in a broad grin. "Myself."

Harry Judson nudged me. "Kit," he said. "Go bring up another couple of bottles from the cellar."

...

What brings a man like Braddock to a place like Litton's Hollow? He was—as he made sure to remind us—an internationally recognized celebrity. He had hunted more legendary beasts than you could shake an elephant gun at, from the megaconda of the Amazon to the Mongolian death worm, from the camel-eating spiders of the Gobi to the Broad-Finned Bear-Whale. He had visited five continents, signed his name to a dozen books, and been romantically linked to four heiresses, a lady explorer, and the daughter of an Austrian count.

Litton's Hollow, on the other hand, was the kind of place that mapmakers tended to leave off their maps to save themselves some work: seventy or eighty houses, most little more than rough-hewn log cabins, nestled on the edge of a hundred square miles of swampland. The people were trappers, fishermen, farmers, or miners. At the time that Braddock visited, we had one saloon, one church, one doctor, and few prospects.

Braddock took his time about enlightening us. The evening wore on, the bottles emptied, and the weaker members of the company slumped to the floor or stumbled outside to vomit. But after an extensive review of his exploits—military, venatory, amatory—he came at last to the point. Between sips of moonshine, he revealed that he had come to do something extraordinary. It was a feat never before attempted, much less accomplished, but he, Whitmore Braddock, aimed to be the first man to pull it off.

He was here to capture a wicker.

...

Ask the average sophisticated citizen of New York or Chicago, and he will tell you that wickers are legendary, the fruit of superstition or the drunken imaginings of a few illiterate hillbillies. Some people might have heard of them. No one believes in them.

Braddock planned to change all that. His goal was nothing less than to capture a living wicker and deliver it to the Barnum Circus, to be exhibited to the awed public as a testimony to the unparalleled manliness, courage, and raw strength of Whitmore J. Braddock, Esq.

There was a lot of shaking of heads at that. Bear-whales are one thing, everyone agreed, but wickers are something else again.

There's something deeply eerie about them. Working the swamps, you'll sometimes see a ragged shape in the misty light that filters down through the gnarled branches of the trees. Picture a tall tangle of sticks, like a pile of brush walking with a gait something like that of a man, glimpsed only out of the corner of your eye as it fades in and out of the mist. Wicker men, an early settler called them, and the name stuck.

They can be killed, more or less. A rifle won't do it—they have no vital spots you could name. Dynamite might do the job. The best tool, though, would be something like a felling axe. The problem is that you need to be as strong and quick as they are, which is a tall order. It's not just that the damned things are inhumanly fast and horrifyingly strong. It's not even their six-foot reach, or the six-inch claws that can gut a cow. It's more that they don't seem to inhabit space in the same way that we do.

No one knows what they really are, not even the Clackamas elders. They were here before the white man came, and probably before the red as well, and they will likely be here after we're gone.

To see a wicker is to be reminded that men are not, after all, the masters of this continent. For all our churches and railroads, our banks and steel mills, there are things here that take no account of us: sasquatches and wendigos, bakaaks, and mishubishu and all the other ancient denizens of lake and forest. And the Clackamas claim that the wickers are the oldest of them all.

...

The next day, we saw the ugly side of Braddock's character.

He rose around two, pale and red-eyed. He had proven his boast: he had outlasted everyone else, putting away a quantity of whisky that would have downed a bull elephant, but the feat had taken its toll.

It was nearly five before he felt well enough to start trying to recruit helpers for his project. When he did, no one wanted anything to do with it. Men who had drunk his whiskey the night before shook their heads and backed away.

By the fifth refusal, Braddock's good humor was wearing thin. By the tenth, he turned nasty.

"I see how it is," he snapped. "A town of mice, not men. Well, I'd rather hunt alone than hunt with cowards." He sat down at the bar and snapped his fingers for whisky.

The mood in the saloon that night was very different from the night before. A few sycophants still hung around Braddock as he held court at the bar. The others gathered in sullen groups in the corners of the room, muttering amongst themselves.

About nine, Braddock turned over his glass and went out to check on the things he had stowed in the back of our storeroom—bales of camping gear, a patent tent, and a steamer trunk as tall as a man. The locals finished their drinks and slipped away. Soon the only person left was Sophie, our local "soiled dove." She waited patiently until Braddock returned, then went upstairs with him. As I blew out the lanterns and banked the fire, I heard the bed-springs in Braddock's room beginning to squeak in protest.

...

True to his word, Braddock went out alone early the next day, poling an old boat that Sammy Henderson had rented to him for not much more than four times the going rate. He worked it handily enough, pushing the boat through the silver water with powerful, economical strokes. A small crowd of curious onlookers gathered to watch, lingering by the dock until he vanished from sight among the mist-shrouded pines.

He reappeared in the evening, just as the light was starting to fail, tied the boat to the dock and sprang ashore, whistling happily.

"Good hunting?" someone called out.

"Good enough," he said. "Saw a couple of wickers, but they were too small, so I let them be." He laughed loudly at his own joke, hefted his gear on his shoulder, and headed for the saloon.

...

It was on the third night that I discovered Braddock's secret.

Braddock had set out early again, returned late, and gone straight to the saloon. Relations with the townsfolk were cordial again, helped by his willingness to stand a round. Say what you like about Braddock, he spent freely, and his money was always good.

I was in the storeroom fetching some cured pork, when a noise from the back caught my ear. I pushed aside the tarpaulin that divided the room—Braddock had been insistent on hiding his stores from curious eyes—and stopped dead.

By the back door, lit obliquely by the moonlight filtering in through the window, stood a wicker. Its head scraped the low ceiling, and its jet-black eyes reflected the flame of the lantern I held. How I did not drop that lantern in fright and set the place ablaze, I will never know.

With my eyes on the wicker, I almost failed to notice that I was not alone. But a movement caught my eye, and I saw the woman.

She was very tall, thin as a rail, wearing only her shift and a pair of gray longjohns. As I watched, she slowly raised and lowered one leg, then raised the other with equal slowness.

I must have gasped involuntarily, because she turned then and saw me. She seemed oblivious to the danger she was in.

"Don't move, ma'am," I begged her, eying the deadly creature in the corner.

She glanced to her right. Instead of shrieking, she smiled. Unfolding gracefully from her pose, she stepped across the room until she was standing next to the wicker.

"Oh, he won't hurt me." she said. "We're old friends." She poked the monster familiarly in the chest. It did not budge. "See?" she said. "Tame as a lamb."

Disbelieving, I took a step forward, and the illusion fell apart.

...

Braddock had done his research. The suit was a masterpiece. Even from less than a foot away—and who would dare come that close?—it could pass for the real thing.

The acrobat, whose name was Carlotta, showed me how she put it on. She explained the complicated system of levers that worked the terrible jaws and flexed the long clawed hands. She showed me the hidden reserve of water that kept the eyes gleamingly moist. Every detail was perfect.

I thought at first it was a lure, but then I understood. "You," I said. "You're the wicker he's going to capture."

She nodded. "He may be a rogue," she said. "But he's not a fool." She looked sad for a moment. "Now you know, what will you do? Will you tell everyone?"

I thought about it. Finally I shook my head. As I understood it, Braddock's deception was being practiced mainly on the rich folks back east who had funded his expedition, not on us. It almost made me like him.

"Thank you," she said. She sighed. "I suppose he's with that doxy again now."

I opened my mouth to say that Sophie wasn't a doxy, then closed it. A doxy was precisely what she was. I nodded.

Carlotta sighed again. "As I said, a rogue. And maybe a fool after all."

...

The capture took place the next day. When Braddock reappeared at dusk, the bow of his boat was filled with the hirsute mass of the fake wicker.

Even knowing it for a fake, I found it hard not to be deceived. The creature—Carlotta!—fought against the bonds that held it, snapping its jaws and carving the air with its talons. Not even the boldest onlookers dared to come within six feet as Braddock dragged the creature down the dock by its chain. When its feet touched dry land, the conflict exploded anew. Man and monster were locked in a brutal dance, and it took all of Braddock's muscle to contain the wild energy of the beast. He was sweating by the time he finally wrestled it into the holding cell that had been prepared for it and fastened its chain to a ringbolt in the wall.

When he turned around, we saw he was bleeding. A red furrow ran over his cheek where one of the claws must have caught him during the mock struggle. He patted his cheek and inspected his fingertips.

The sight of his own blood seemed to enrage him. Before anyone could stop him, he snatched up an oar and ran it through the barred window, stabbing at the captive within. I was not the only one who heard the human cry of pain from inside.

"Cruel," said a voice from the crowd. "Cruel to treat a living thing so."

Braddock glowered at the speaker. "What business is it of yours, you old Indian witch?"

There was a murmur at that, and the crowd drew back slightly. Someone reached out to touch Granny Vala's shoulder, but she shook the hand off angrily, muttering in her own language.

Braddock took a step toward her. The old woman stood her ground, unintimidated. He bent down until his face was only inches away from hers.

"Mine," he said. "Mine to do what I like with. Understand?"

She held his gaze for a moment, then turned away, shaking her head.

Braddock watched her hobble away. He turned to his circle of admirers. "Drinks," he said. "Everyone drinks on me tonight."

...

There was a full moon that night, and the boughs of the forest were tangled black and silver.

I lay in my room under the eaves, unable to sleep. On the floor below, Braddock snored thunderously. I got up and walked barefoot to the window.

A hunched figure was sitting at the end of the dock, fingertips trailing in the water. When the snoring subsided for a moment, the night breeze carried me snatches of chanting, strange sounds in an eerie burbling, clicking dialect that seemed less like human speech than the sighing of the marsh wind among the dead trees. Braddock never heard any part of it. And he never heard when, a scant hour before dawn, something answered from far out in the swamp.

...

I was in the crowd the next morning when Braddock led his captive down the main street toward the waiting stage. In the light of day, the creature looked larger and wilder than ever, but a night in captivity must have broken its spirit. It followed him obediently, head lowered, clawed hands held demurely by its sides. As for Braddock, his eyes might be red from the excesses of the previous night, but he still looked every inch a conqueror. He swaggered and strode, his sideburns like clumps of Spanish moss, the knives at his belt gleaming in the weak morning light.

Braddock had done his research. The perfection of the suit was proof of that. But somehow it never occurred to him to wonder how it was that we could live as we did on the edges of a swamp inhabited by such deadly and unpredictable creatures. Thus he never had any notion of the delicate balance that rules our lives or of the role that even seemingly insignificant figures play in our community. And, irony of ironies, he never knew how close to the mark he was when he called Granny Vala an "old witch."

Or perhaps he did. Perhaps, in his last moments, he realized his mistake. Because as he tugged on the chain once more, he looked up and saw the acrobat, tall and pale in her gray dress. I was close enough to see her smile coldly at him, a smile duplicated by the diminutive old woman at her side. And in that final second, I saw the fatal question flicker across his face.

If she's over there, who's in the suit?

###

About the Author

Angus McIntyre's short fiction has appeared in the anthologies *Mission: Tomorrow, Humanity 2.0,* and *Swords & Steam,* in *Abyss and Apex* and *Black Candies* magazines, and on the BoingBoing website. Another story will appear in *Lovecraft eZine*. His novella, *The Warrior Within,* has been acquired for 2017 by Tor.com.

*****~~~~~*****

The Groks of Kruk County

by Columbkill Noonan

"Gimme a coin," demanded Cron, flapping his long scaly fingers impatiently at his woman like a small hatchling demanding a treat.

If said woman, whose name was Auda, minded, or even noticed, the rudeness of the gesture, she said nothing. Instead she hurriedly handed over the copper coin. She, too, was in a hurry for Cron to finish what he was doing, and the coin was an important part of the last step.

To her mind, a bit of rudeness here and there was a small price to pay for the end result of what Cron was currently working on. As long as he finished quickly, he could talk to her any way he liked, as far as she was concerned.

What Cron was doing was cooking up a giant spoonful of crup. He held the spoon over a lit torch held between his knobby knees, so that the fluid within bubbled and smoked. Auda licked her lips at the caustic smell of it, as if anticipating a tasty treat.

They had been smoking crup all night (which was, in truth, what they did most nights). Just a few minutes ago, however, they had run out, which was why Cron was cooking up a new batch now.

"Hurry up, will ya?" urged Auda, leaning forward to look closely at the thin white film that had formed on the surface of the mixture.

The ingredients of crup were the roots of crupinga weed, targot poison, and water. The first two ingredients nearly always proved fatal when ingested by themselves (and, quite often, even when cooked up together according to the traditional recipe that Cron was following now). This was, however, a matter of no consequence to folk such as Cron and Auda, who were so addicted to the crup that no amount of death could deter them from smoking it.

"If it gets too hot. . . " warned Auda.

"Shut up, already, willya?" snipped Cron. "Like I ain't done it a million times."

He shook his head as he slowly, gently dragged the coin across the top of the bubbling crup. The white part at the top (which was, theoretically at least, the crup that was safe to smoke; the poisonous parts ought to have sunk to the bottom by now) stuck to the coin. Cron carefully, almost reverently, wiped it off on a plate before returning the coin to the spoon to collect more.

Auda reached for the stuff on the plate, but Cron smacked her hand away. "Wait for me," he commanded. "I ain't doing this just so's you can smoke it all and me have none, am I?"

"Well, hurry up then!" said Auda impatiently.

Auda was having a hard time waiting for the crup to be ready, because crup was highly addictive. Once someone started on crup they wanted more. If a Grok smoked crup once, or maybe twice, then they always wanted to smoke it again.

But Cron and Auda didn't care about that, or even think about it. They wanted more, and they wanted it now. Such was the nature of the crup, and such was the nature of Groks such as Cron and Auda.

Crup smoking was a problem that plagued what was considered the dregs of Grok society, and therefore wasn't given too much thought by the rest of the Groks. Cron and Auda were part of not only that lower level of society, but also of the lower rung of that lower level. No one really cared about them, and they didn't really care about anyone in turn. Or any*thing*, really, except for the crup.

Cron and Auda were part of a population of Groks who inhabited a mountainous, remote region of the country. The place was called Kruk County, and here lived small-time farmers, crup dealers, and crup addicts, and not much else. The Groks here were derisively referred to as "Mountain Groks" by the snobby lowlanders, whenever they deigned to notice them.

Mountain Groks tended to be a paler shade of green than their more sophisticated urban brethren who lived in the lowland cities. It seemed that inbreeding among Groks (who, in fairness, suffered from such low populations that achieving sufficient genetic diversity in a mate was challenging if not entirely impossible) resulted in a lack of pigment production. While city Groks tended to be a deep, emerald green, many of the Mountain Groks were lime green or sage green or even snot green.

Cron and Auda happened to be two of the palest Groks around. They did nothing to dispel the prejudices against their kind; indeed, they did much to support them instead.

At last Cron had finished collecting the last of the crup from the spoon. He scooped it all together and stuffed it into a pipe and handed it to Auda along with the lit torch.

This, thought Auda as she inhaled, scarcely noticing that the torch had gotten too close to her face and was singeing off her eyelashes, was the life. A man who gave you the first hit of the crup pipe was a man worth keeping, and he was all hers. She had crup, and she had true love, and she had goks aplenty to steal, and who could want for anything more?

Goks were eight-legged hairy creatures that Mountain Groks rode to get themselves from one place to another. Sadly, they were a bit expensive, so that only the richest of the Mountain Groks could actually afford to own one.

Cost, of course, was no impediment to Groks like Cron and Auda, who were clever and suffered from no pesky moral consciences. If they had to go somewhere, they could simply steal a gok and ride it wherever they wanted.

Or, if they ran out of money to buy crup, they could steal a gok and sell it on the sly (there was no lack of buyers in these parts for stolen goks; no one asked where a gok came from as long as the price was right).

As Cron and Auda passed the pipe back and forth and watched the crup quickly disappear whilst they were still far from feeling sated, they both came to the same conclusion. It was Cron who voiced it first.

"Well, I s'pose we'd best go steal ourselves a gok, don'tchya think?" he said.

"Ayup," said Auda. "How 'bout from Brub up the hill? He's got a whole lot of new goks up there. Prolly wouldn't even notice if'n a couple went gone."

"I dunno," said Cron. "Brub seemed like he knew somethin' was up the last time we got one of his. He's mighty suspicious-like." He sounded resentful, as though Brub had somehow wronged them by rightfully suspecting that Cron and Auda were gok thieves.

"He's a son of a bitch, ain't he?" said Auda. "I says we take the whole durned herd!"

"Yeah!" said Cron, his prudent reservations forgotten in the haze of the crup and the face of Auda's vehemence. "Let's do it! All of 'em!"

And so Cron and Auda crept out of the tiny shack that they called home and crept up quietly to the field where their neighbor Brub kept his herd of goks.

Their idea of quiet, however, was far different from anyone else's, so high were they on the crup, so that they actually made quite a racket as they blundered up the hill. So much noise did they make that Brub knew they were coming long before they arrived, and was ready for them.

Brub picked up a big, heavy shovel and hid himself behind a tree. He waited until Cron and Auda had clumsily climbed over his fence and taken hold of one of his goks (murder was, after all, a crime, but gok stealing was a worse one, and a Grok was in his rights to do whatever he liked to anyone he caught stealing one from him). Then, he walked up behind them and said, "Hey," just as casually as you please.

Cron and Auda turned around at the sound of his voice, and Brub, tired of the two of them stealing his goks, struck them calmly, one after the other, in the face with his shovel. Then, first checking to make sure that they were dead, he walked off and left them there to rot in the field, pleased that they would steal his goks no more.

"Cron?" said Auda at last, her voice sounding odd even to her own ears, which were still ringing from the sound of the shovel impacting with her tough skull. "Are we dead?"

"Well," said Cron. He looked down at himself and saw that he was translucent. Then he looked over towards Auda and saw that she, too, was completely transparent. Also, their more solid, corporeal bodies still lay on the ground with their heads caved in most unpleasantly, while their new, filmy bodies were floating a few feet above. "I reckon that we are."

"But this is terrible!" wailed Auda. "How will we get the crup if we're dead?"

"Huh," said Cron, thinking. As he thought, a gok walked up behind him, and nudged him out of the way.

"Hey, did that gok just push you?" asked Auda shrewdly.

"What of it?" snapped Cron grumpily. "Like it's not enough I'm dead with a shovel in the face, but you gotta make fun of me too?"

"No, stupid," said Auda happily. "I mean, if the *gok* could touch *you*, then *you* could touch *it*, right?"

"Well, duh!" said Cron. "Course I can."

"So we can still steal goks!" chirped Auda. "Which means we can still smoke crup. Only now no body's gonna see us, so we can do it all we want."

"You're a genius, woman!" cried Cron. "Let's go see!"

They tested Auda's theory, first floating on into Brub's house to look for his stash of crup. It seemed that he couldn't see them at all, so after they found it they smoked it right in front of him, so that he could see the pipe floating around and the smoke coming out of it but couldn't figure out what was going on. Brub ran about in a panic as he watched his precious crup disappear. Cron and Auda, now happily high again, laughed and laughed as they flitted out of Brub's house followed by the sound of their murderer's cries of dismay.

"Now let's see if we can steal a gok!" said Cron. They laid their now-filmy hands on the nearest gok and managed to tie a rope around it. They led the beast out of the field and all the way down to a place where stolen goks could be bought and sold, crowing with delight at their success.

Of course, once there, they couldn't actually sell the gok, since nobody could see them. Still, most of the fun was in the sneaking and stealing and mischief of the whole thing. Besides, since they could now simply float in to anyplace and smoke all the crup they wanted for free, they had no real need for money anyway, and they were satisfied.

And so it went on for years and decades and centuries, with the spirits of Cron and Auda terrorizing generation upon generation of Mountain Groks in Kruk

County. They stole people's crup, cooked it up, and smoked it until they thought they'd OD (which of course wasn't a worry for them, not anymore now that they were dead anyway). And though they had no need to steal people's goks (since ghosts have no need of money and wouldn't know what to do with it if they had any), being ornery sorts they still enjoyed doing it.

Countless Groks woke up to find their goks missing and their stash of crup gone, with only the acrid smell of smoke hanging in the air to let them know that they had been visited in the night by the dreaded crup-smoking-gok-stealing ghosts of Cron and Auda. But, being Mountain Groks and thus none too bright, no one ever thought of anything to do about it, so that Cron and Auda were sure that they could go on this way forever.

Until, that is, the arrival of the humans. Great big metal flying things appeared in the sky one day, and before any Grok could think to even wonder what they were, strange little pink people came spewing out of them.

The Groks laughed for a moment at the sight of them, so tiny and small and smooth-skinned, like talking worms with legs. But then the humans saw the Groks and pointed little metal sticks at them, which made big bangs that somehow opened terrible holes in the Groks' bodies.

Soon enough, all of the Groks in Kruk County were gone (either killed by the nasty noisy sticks of the humans or herded off to work as slaves who-knows-where. All of the Groks, that is, except for Cron and Auda.

"Whaddew we do now?" wailed Auda, when she saw that not only were all the Groks gone but that the creepy little humans apparently had no need for crup. With no Groks there was no crup; it was as simple as that, and Cron and Auda were in a terrible fix because of it.

"Well, we can still steal goks," said Cron, trying to cheer Auda up even though he too was desperately unhappy at the prospect of facing eternity here in a place that no longer had any crup. He could already feel the withdrawal tremors coursing through his ghostly body and a terrible agitation building in his brain, and he guessed that things would only get worse as time went on.

"I guess," said Auda doubtfully, scratching at the phantom itches that danced away from her chasing fingers. But even as she said it she knew that even the joy of gok-stealing couldn't come close to the feeling of that first puff of crup.

Even so, they went out that night to try, hoping that it would distract them from their misery a little bit at least. They stole a good number of goks, but in the morning it seemed that the horrible little humans couldn't have cared less. In truth, the goks looked quite a bit like giant spiders to the humans, and therefore they were a bit relieved to wake up to find that so many of them had disappeared.

Cron and Auda were enraged.

"Can you even believe it?" shrieked Auda, in a fine temper. "We musta took a whole herd of goks, and ain't nobody even cared at all!"

"They must be stupid, or something," said Cron. "Din't even *try* to look for 'em, did they?"

"Not at all!" said Auda. "It ain't even fun if nobody done cares." She pouted hideously, her warty lower lip protruding well past her upper fangs.

Seeing his woman so upset infuriated Cron even further. "If they won't be upset about the goks," he yelled, "well then, we'll give 'em something to be upset about!"

"Yeah!" cried Auda, jumping to her feet. "Uh, what'll we give 'em?"

Cron thought for a few long moments. "We'll go wreck stuff!" he proclaimed at last. Auda whooped, and together they went out in search of stuff to wreck.

The first thing they came upon was a large building. It was long and low, with a big squared-off tower in the front from which protruded an odd structure that consisted of two wooden planks stuck together so that it looked to Cron and Auda a bit like an "X" tilted over on its side.

"In here!" said Cron. "Sounds like there's a whole lot of the wretches in there. Singin', and what-not."

"Tons of 'em," agreed Auda. "I want to scare them until they all die, Cron. Till they die!"

"Then that's what we gonna do," said Cron. And they entered the church in order to do just that.

As soon as they passed over the threshold they began shrieking and throwing things and generally making a terrible ruckus. At first the people screamed and yelled and tried to run away. "Ghosts! Devils!" they yelled, and though Cron and Auda had no idea what those things were they thought they sounded very scary indeed, and were pleased.

Soon, however, one human stepped forward. He wore long white robes and a big pointy hat atop his head.

"I'm gonna grab that stupid hat," said Auda, "and pull it off his stupid pink head."

"Careful," warned Cron. "That might be where he keeps his crup. Anybody who would wear a hat that stupid has gotta be high, right?"

"Right!" agreed Auda. She went over to the human in question and carefully yanked the hat from his head. Looking inside and finding it empty of crup, she began beating the fellow about the head with it.

To Cron and Auda's surprise, the human didn't react with fear, or panic, or by running away. Instead, he reached into a pocket in his robe and pulled out a vial of water.

"What's that?" Auda asked Cron, watching with confusion as the man held the vial out in front of him like a weapon.

"I don't rightly know," said Cron, frowning. "Maybe it's their kind of crup? Liquid crup?"

"Prolly!" chirped Auda. "And he's gonna give it to us to make us stop, I bet." She moved closer to the vial, trying to sniff it.

To her surprise, the human jerked back the arm that held the vial, then flung it forward so that drops of it flew out and landed right in Auda's face. "The Power of Christ compels you!" yelled the human nonsensically.

"What?" said Auda, then yelped as the drops hit her skin. They burned, and she wiped furiously at them to get them off.

"What's he sayin'" asked Cron, coming up closer to investigate. He hadn't noticed Auda's discomfort from the fluid, and therefore was close enough to her to be hit by the drops the second time the human shook the vial at Auda. "Ack!" cried Cron.

"What is it?" cried Auda. "It burns!"

"I think my skin's coming off," said Cron, patting frantically at his face where the drops had landed.

"In the name of the Father, the Son, and the Holy Spirit, I command you!" intoned the human in a terrible sonorous voice. The words, which made no sense whatsoever to Cron and Auda, nonetheless seemed to hit them like a physical blow, sending them caroming backwards away from the nasty human. Another spray of the awful fluid followed, so that they both squealed in pain.

"It's making me feel kinda fuzzy," said Auda. "Like I'm disappearing a little."

"Me too," said Cron. "Run!"

The frighteners had become the frightened, it seemed. Cron turned tail and ran, and Auda did the same. The human, however, seemed to give chase and kept chanting strange words and flinging the strange liquid all around as they ran, so that soon they were both doused.

Auda's strength gave out, and she fell. Cron managed a few more steps before he did the same. The words and the burning water combined were doing what they were designed to do, which was, of course, to exorcise unwanted spirits.

"I think I'm fading," said Auda. "I can't even see myself so good anymore."

"Urgh," said Cron, who was also starting to disappear.

"Why couldn't they just have some decent crup?" bemoaned Auda.

"If this is crup, then I don't think I like it anymore," agreed Cron, before he and Auda both gave in to the holy water and words of exorcism.

And so it was that the spirits of Cron and Auda were gotten rid of at last, and went wherever it is that bad Mountain Groks go, and haunted Kruk County no more.

###

About the Author

Columbkill Noonan has an M.S. in Biology, and lives in Baltimore, Maryland. She teaches Anatomy and Physiology at a university in Maryland.

In her spare time, Columbkill enjoys hiking, aerial yoga, and riding her horse, Mittens. To learn more about Columbkill, please feel free to visit her on Twitter @ColumbkillNoon1.

*****~~~~~*****

Mourning Dove

by Jackson Kuhl

Nothing but dust and tumbleweeds passed before the horses of Jed Vega and his gang of outlaws as they rode through the streets of Mourning Dove. But when they arrived downtown at the La Canela, there in front stood a grim-faced old man, surrounded by his wife and presumably several children and grandchildren. The wife and some of the rest were crying.

"Usually the women weep when we *leave* town, not when we arrive," Vega said to the man mounted beside him, whose name was Tom Berger. Berger laughed. The others laughed. They all had a good laugh, except for the old man and his family.

Vega leaned forward on his saddle horn. "Tell me, old-timer: for what reason is this lamentation? Is our reputation so bad you cry at first sight of me and my associates?"

"They don't lament what you have done, Jed Vega," said the man, "But rather what you will do. Tomorrow you will shoot me dead in this street. That's why my family grieves."

Berger and the rest chuckled but Vega frowned. "Why would I shoot an unarmed coot like you? I shoot up banks, not long-toothed graybeards. Unless you mean to cross me in some fashion."

The old man shook his head. "I won't cross you. In fact after this moment you and I will never exchange words again. You will head into the La Canela, and afterwards proceed to the newspaper office. As for me, I will wait here for daybreak, when I will die."

Vega and the members of his gang exchanged looks. "If the rest of the townsfolk are half as loco as this bunch," said Berger, "The bank manager might as well hand us his key ring right now."

"Maybe," said Vega. "But before we get to the matter of thieving, we need to attend to the matter of quenching." He dismounted and wrapped his reins around the hitching bar.

Beyond the bat-wing doors of the La Canela the player piano jangled a jig to a nearly empty saloon. The bar man stood waiting for them, a bottle and five glasses set upon the polished pecan.

"Good afternoon, gentlemen," he said. "I've saved a bottle of your favorite whiskey just for you, Mr. Vega." He poured the Kessler into the glassware.

Again the riders traded glances, more darkly than before. Vega eyed the saloon keeper narrowly and didn't touch his glass. For a perfect stranger to openly declare Vega's fondness for Kessler's over straight bourbon was an arrow too close to the bull's-eye. "I reckon our notoriety has gotten ahead of us, boys. That's not good."

"Means they'll be waiting for us over at the First Federal," said Jim Williamson.

"Indeed it suggests just that." Vega smiled at the bar man. Then quick as a cottonmouth he grabbed him by the throat and pulled him halfway over the bar top. "What I want to know is how anyone in this dead-horse burg knew we were coming, when we ourselves only decided to visit yesterday?"

The keeper recognized that an answer was expected of him regardless of his ability to breathe. He sucked in air and made the best of a reply. "*Your arrival—the newspaper.*"

Vega cocked his head. "Are you saying everyone knew we were coming to town because they read it in the *newspaper*?"

The bar man nodded.

Vega released him, knocked back his glass of whiskey.

"All right here, Mr. Vega." The keeper handed him a broadsheet. "The morning edition."

Vega indicated his empty glass and shook out the paper while the barkeep filled. There it was, in black and off-white, under the headline, "Notorious Band of Bank Robbers Arrives to Menace Mourning Dove." He read:

. . . After a brief exchange with old Saul Abbott, the retired ploughman whom Vega would shoot and kill the following morning, the party of wanted men retired to the La Canela, where they imbibed more than two fingers of Vega's favorite label, Kessler Whiskey, before proceeding to the publishing office of this fair missive in due agitation. . .

The article continued in a like vein, but Vega quit reading—everything had become clear in the polished windowpane of his mind. He tossed aside the paper. Berger picked it up and read aloud to the others.

"There's something wrong in this place," said Diego Ramos.

Berger said, "Maybe we should move on to the next town, Jed."

"Can't you see it? They're trying to set a trap, boys." And Vega explained to his associates how simple it would be for the town marshal and his deputized do-gooders to set an ambush by luring the band to some banal spot like, say, a newspaper publisher. It was a good idea, Vega had to admit. All that was needed was a planted stooge in the street and a few hair strands of gossip printed in ink to make the reader think the future had been prophesied; and that by stirring the gang members into consternation about such omens and forecasts, they, the law men, could take Vega's gang unaware when they arrived at the press office to root out the mystery of such Nostradamic newsprint. Somehow the town leaders of Mourning Dove had known Vega and his men had set their sights on the silver in the local vault, and devised an unusual and frankly clever strategem to clap them in chains instead.

As stealthy as panthers, the gang surrounded the newspaper office: Ramos framed in a window across the deserted street, the Williamson brothers by the back, Berger pressing himself flat against the door jamb of the entrance. As they positioned themselves, Vega glanced over his shoulder to see the old man, now alone in the street, watching him in silence.

Vega went in the front, padding softly, Navy Colt drawn. But inside there was no hail of gunfire, no deputies pivoting around corners with barrels blazing. The office was abandoned save for a solitary woman scribbling at a desk. A whirring noise emanated faintly from an uncertain source.

"Oh, you can put away your gun, Mr. Vega," said the woman without looking up. "The marshal left with the rest. There's not a single lawman remaining in Mourning Dove."

Vega wasn't inclined toward trust, but after looking behind a few doors and nudging aside several curtains with the nose of his revolver, he finally holstered it. "And you are?"

The woman turned to him, her face pretty but bony as if a sirocco of hourglass sand had worn away every morsel of fat beneath her skin.

"Lynette Osbourne, publisher and editrix of the *Mourning Dove Standard.*" She returned to her writing.

"You're here to sabotage the printing press. Good luck. My husband stripped every bolt and screw before his departure. Nothing but a bundle of dynamite or a runaway Santa Fe steam engine could destroy it now."

Vega noted the enormous mass of arms and spindles and belts that took up more than half the room, fashioned from cast iron and oiled steel. "Ma'am," he said, "I couldn't give a damn about your press machine. I came here to empty your bank safe and shoot anyone who gets in my way."

"No. That's why you came to *town*. But you've come to *my office* because you're frightened by how the morning edition of my newspaper printed your whereabouts and doings before you ever set foot in the La Canela."

She rose and walked to the press. "My husband started this newspaper to compete with the other established dailies in town. Every one of them printed a single afternoon edition per day. He realized he could gain an advantage by running *two* editions every day, and jump the competition by putting a morning edition on the streets for folks to read while they ate their bacon. But publishing two newspapers every single day is hard work, and doesn't leave time for much else. So he invented this press to write the morning edition for him." She patted the metal. "Thing is, he went ahead and somehow made a machine that wrote news *before* it happened, saving him the trouble of having to write about it afterwards."

Vega knew about printing and newspapers the way horses knew about growing tea in China. And yet he was fairly sure of himself when he said, "There's no way anybody on this Earth could make a machine that writes the future."

"I agree with you, Mr. Vega. That's not what the press does. What my husband did was build a machine that suggests what *might* happen, not what *will* happen, but the results are so close to what actually *does* happen that the two are identical. What is probable or potential becomes real."

"But how?"

She pointed to a boxy portion of the press, one side of which was walled with plate glass. Inside, numerous rolls of paper turned at different speeds. The paper was pierced at intervals.

"It operates like a player piano," said Osbourne, "With the perforations in the paper indicating what words and phrases are printed on the newspaper. The perforations never line up in the same sequence twice, so every evening the press creates an entirely new issue—one that very accurately describes the events of the following day."

"How did he make the paper spools, then? How'd he know where to cut the holes?"

Osbourne shrugged. "I don't know. Nobody does. Upon realizing he had invented his way out of a lifelong career, my husband sat down in this office, put a gun in his mouth, and pulled the trigger. Just like the newspaper said he would."

Realization dawned in Vega, and he sagged.

"That's why everybody left town. Nobody can stand knowing if they're going to catch consumption or be trampled by a horse or go bankrupt. Like prisoners on the eve of execution. Nothing to look forward to, no hope." Which meant they had taken their bank deposits with them. He looked at her. "So, why stay? You and the saloon keeper and the old man in the street?"

Osbourne smiled. "There is a comfort for some in knowing the day and hour of one's demise. If you knew you would die on the morrow, Mr. Vega, how would you spend tonight?" And as the press roared to life in a thunderbolt of pounding and clacking, Osbourne ripped a sheet from the belt and thrust it at Vega.

...

Mourning Dove

When Jed Vega awoke, the room was orange. He blinked, ran a tongue that tasted like baked raccoon over dry lips. He sat up—his stomach lurched. On the nightstand lay an empty tumbler next to a Bowie knife. Disconnected daguerreotypes sputtered past his eyes, images of whiskey bottles and paper spools.

The wind rattled the sashes. Vega walked over and swung open the shutters. A mandarin wall stood beyond the glass. He staggered downstairs to the saloon.

"Dust storm," said the saloon keeper. "Worst Mourning Dove's ever seen. It's all right here." He slid the morning edition and a cup of coffee across the bar. Vega ignored the *Standard*. He was sick, sick from Kessler's and sick of their damn newspaper.

"You must love it," Vega said, "Being told what to do, no better than a heifer in the chute."

The keeper leaned his palms on the pecan. "No, Mr. Vega. I'll tell you what I do enjoy though. I enjoy opening the paper every morning and not seeing my name anywhere in it. If I'm not printed on the pages, or if the names of the people I love most aren't there, then I know nothing particularly bad will happen to any of us that day."

"And nothing good either." Vega slurped the coffee. "You just go through your lives as bland and weak as this coffee."

"There were some in Mourning Dove who would've agreed with you, before they left. But it turns out most prefer *not* knowing what might come, good or bad, even if they say otherwise."

A blast of wind struck the hotel, and the posts groaned.

"Goddamn it." The coffee curdled in Vega's gut. "Me and my boys're stuck in this podunk until the storm clears."

The keeper frowned, a bearer of tidings he was reluctant to deliver. "Mr. Vega, your men left while it was still dark. After you passed out and they carried you to your room."

Vega glared at him.

"It's all right there." He read Vega's face and, pulling at his collar, suddenly decided he needed to retrieve something from the kitchen.

Vega picked up the paper, his pupils too blurry to focus. Without warning the keys of the piano danced up and down, the spool of paper turning, its wires singing. Vega threw his coffee cup at it and stomped out.

Choking on the grit thrown into his face, he stopped to tie his handkerchief across nose and mouth. The bastards had left him because of what the paper had said. Cowards and traitors, all of them—he had always suspected Berger of wanting him out of the gang. He would make it up to them. Vega would destroy the press, destroy that gear works of tricks and lies, then track his former associates. Shoot Berger and horsewhip the rest.

The atmosphere was more sand than air, stinging his eyes, lancing his skin. He couldn't see beyond his fingertips, and like snow on the plains it cascaded into dunes and gullies, tripping him. Vega stumbled through a blank orange canvas, sightless and hobbled, as the grains fell like birdshot around his ears.

Wading through the streets, he came to a crossroads. Something loomed out of the void, an indistinct colossus. It trudged across his path on two legs, footsteps audible, its furry hide striped like a zebra's. Vega froze. The creature swung a toothy head toward him, seeking. But it was just as blinded by the dust as he was. It turned away and trudged off into the gloom.

For a moment Vega stood dumbfounded, waiting for it to return, wondering if it had been a vision spun from the storm. The sand accumulated around his ankles and calves. He shook his feet loose and walked on.

Like an Egyptian temple, the columns of a storefront rose out of the opacity. Vega recognized it. The newspaper office wasn't far. He ran, jumped through the drifts to the raised boardwalk, grasped the knob.

A squealing mass of wings and India rubber pinned him against the door. Instinctively Vega shoved it away, but it stuck to him with suckered claws, its cabbage head a mass of clutching tentacles. It strained for his face, Vega pushing it away with his forearm across its neck. He screamed, and the creature screamed back, drawing him closer. He inched his right arm down his side, found his Colt, bent and fired it still half in the leather. The beast leapt into an updraft and was swallowed by the sand.

Gasping, Vega stumbled into the street, his pistol raised. Hunting.

It lurched at him sideways, an old face of hair and baleful eyes. Vega fired. Saul Abbott grunted and fell dead to the ground.

He found Lynette Osbourne standing by the printing press, head bowed in contemplation.

"I'm going to destroy that infernal machine once and for all," said Vega.

"Didn't you do that last night?" Osbourne asked. "When you showed up here drunk and attacked it with your knife?"

Vega stopped. A dull recollection returned to him.

She pointed. "The rolls. The paper rolls. You cut them. Perforated them."

The pane of glass in the printing press had been shattered. Inside their box, the various spools still whirred, but the paper was now gashed and ripped and torn, the wounds ugly beside the cleanly cut rectangles of the original perforations. It came back to him, then: a plan, formed deep inside the whiskey midnight, to alter the spools and rewrite what could be. A future where Vega never needed to rob banks again—because their gold and silver and notes already belonged to him.

"The newspaper said nothing about that. The copy you gave me."

Osbourne looked at him. "There was a third edition—a *late* edition. After you left here to spend your last hours with your whiskey and your knife. It's never done that before, but then again, it's never been attacked by a madman before."

Vega gestured at the ocher glow outside the glass. "The monsters."

"Yes. What was only potential in history and in nature is now become physical. Because of your handiwork."

Vega had no response. The door shook on its hinges. "And still you stay here."

"Why do you rob banks, Mr. Vega?"

"I got to live. I got to eat. I could never stand taking orders from some foreman or breaking my back so somebody else could grow rich."

"That's a story you tell yourself. You rob banks because like everyone else, you don't know what the next day brings. So we assume we *have* to work to feed and shelter ourselves, to grow food or pursue our profession or even steal. But what a gift it is to know for certain whether we *have* to do those things or if we can surrender them altogether."

She walked over to him, pulled a Shopkeeper Special from her dress pocket. "It was a gift from my husband to the world. A gift you have stolen from Mourning Dove. Stolen from *me*."

Slowly Vega lowered his hands toward his gun belt. "You don't want to get into a shootout, little lady. We both know who will win."

"Do we know anything now, either of us?" She motioned with the barrel toward a copy of the *Standard* on a desk beside him. "What does the paper say?"

Vega didn't move.

"Pick it up."

Still he waited.

Osbourne cocked the hammer.

"*Pick it up*."

Vega did so, reluctant to fill his open hands.

"What does the newspaper say will happen?"

Vega looked down at the print and read. The sand gusted at the door. His intestines sank.

###

About the Author

Jackson Kuhl is a writer in Connecticut.

*****~~~~~*****

Willing

by Premee Mohamed

Bought bred, the new cow had cost three thousand dollars, and so as night fell with no sign of the calf, it was Arnold himself who trudged back and forth between the house and the barn, waving away the hired hands. "My money," he grunted. "My problem." A storm struck up, not snow but a roaring haze of fine sleet that crusted his beard with ice. Far to the west, visible only by their bluish, luminous heat, the old gods of grass and grain bayed to the cloud-buried stars. Arnold ignored them. It was too early in the year for a sacrifice.

On the fifth trip, his youngest child joined him, silent as ever, silvery hair greased down from the rain, in her oldest brother's canvas coat. She liked their ancient hand-me-downs, though she was so small that everything trailed in the muck like the train of a wedding dress. Over the splattering slush Arnold heard her rubber boots squelching in the wallow that had been the path. He waited for her to catch up before continuing to the barn.

The new cow had finally bedded herself for labour; Arnold checked the others, finding another at the far end who looked ready. Often happened like that, several at once. They huffed softly as he passed, as if remarking on what a cold night it was, and how pleasant the new ceramic heaters were.

"There's gonna be two babies tonight," Arnold said as he returned to the half-open barn door. "So you better go back to the house."

"I'm not cold."

"I don't want you in the way when it's go-time," he clarified. "Crying or whatnot."

"I'm not afraid of the blood."

He gave up. "Well, let's just wait, then." She doffed the wet coat and climbed onto a bale, only her eyes and a few pale curls visible in the low light. Strange critter, this one. She never called him "Daddy," never reached for his hand while they walked, listened to him so carefully that he stuttered into silence in the face of that expectant vacuum. As if she weren't his child at all, but some over-friendly neighbour's kid, a regular visitor who happened to like cows and chickens and listening to the old man talk. Twenty-four years between her and her next sibling, when Arnold and Marla had believed all that behind them. And then in what seemed the space of moments, it was diapers again, and bottles, and covering the outlets, and hand-me-ups from her own nieces and nephews. Not for the first time, Arnold thought that perhaps she should have been sent to live with one of them—safe in the city, instead of out here with two farmers pushing sixty, and a rotating crew of hired hands too busy to watch for a kid underfoot.

The new Simmental's glossy coat heaved as she worked to get the calf out, birthwaters flowing through the fresh hay and down the drain. Arnold wasn't worried; her papers said she'd already had two calves, the second almost a hundred pounds. The wind battering the cinderblock walls drowned out the cow's steady, heavy breathing, her placid moans. Yes, money well spent.

"What about the other one?" Clover said.

"I'll go check on her in a minute," Arnold said, but feeling the pressure of the child's eyes from her dark corner, added, "All right, you go. Stall 18."

She slid off her hay bale and pattered down the dimly lit corridor, returning at speed far too soon. "Something's wrong!" she gasped.

"All right. Stay here." That's farming, he wanted to explain. Something always goes wrong. You're too little to know it yet, that's all. But in a few years you'll catch yourself saying it over all sorts of things—boys, school, crooked fence posts. Something *always* goes wrong. And then we fix it. That's how it works.

But the cow was dead, bled out so silently and completely that for the stunned space of a minute all Arnold could think was that she'd been shot, even scanning the flawless walls for a bullet-pock, for there seemed to be no other way it could have happened so fast. Blood gurgled down the drain as he let himself into the stall and picked up the soaked, shivering calf. Its small head lolled in the crook of his arm as he carried it to the med room for a wash and warm, the fluorescents blinding after the cosy amber lights. He sensed rather than saw his daughter's presence in the doorway.

"Run back to the house," he said. "And get some blankets from your mama, OK?"

"Did the cow—"

"Blankets," he said.

But when she returned, dragging a muddy garbage bag full of bedding, the Simmental had also delivered—a stillbirth monstrosity. Arnold squatted in the hay, staring at the thing. Item one: He'd get back some of that three thousand dollars. How much would be up to Crutchfield or his agents, but he'd argue for half. Item two: The calf who had survived its birth, trembling, hungry and alone. Item three. . . item. . .

"What happened to it?" Clover whispered. "Was it the gods?"

Arnold wasn't listening. Well. Not a disaster. It'd happened before, hadn't it? The only problem was the girl; but if she hadn't fallen apart on seeing the carnage in Stall

18, she'd be fine now. "Wrap it up warm," he said, gesturing at the black-and-white calf. "Gotta clean this up."

But even with the twisted and truncated remains of her dead calf gone, and the stall hosed down and loaded with fresh hay, the Simmental bit and kicked at the interloper, refusing access to teats so visibly heavy that Arnold felt ghost pains of his own. He scratched what was left of his hair through his hat, thinking.

"She doesn't *love* her," Clover said tremulously, arms fastened around the calf's neck.

"Well, cows, see," Arnold began, and trailed off. World harsh enough tonight. Gods abroad, and a storm raging, and the girl just seven, not even double digits, two columns in the accounting book. There was one more thing to try. Worked a couple of seasons ago, if he recalled rightly. "Go stand in the hallway for a minute."

Even anointed with the monstrosity's afterbirth, though, the calf made no headway; Arnold swooped it out of the way before its skull got stove in. Desperate times. This next step he would certainly not allow the child to watch, and he locked the door on the med room before getting out the scalpel. "Well, I'm sorry," he muttered to the bewildered calf. "It ain't your fault. It's a smell thing. Not your fault. Pull this off and maybe you'll get breakfast out of it. Deal? Deal."

The stillbirth was a pain to skin, great cysts of clear fluid popping and flexing under its hide as he worked to free a big enough piece. He draped it over the calf, tied a few raggedy flaps as best he could, and brought it back to the Simmental. He and Clover watched in silence as the cow sniffed the calf—a pitiful thing next to her majestic bulk—and then slowly, thoroughly, began to lick it. Outside, something emitted a long, ghostly wail, whether of despair or triumph Arnold wasn't sure.

Back at the house, he crumbled a handful of summer sage into a dish of milk and put it out on the doorstep as thanks, braving a moment's slap of rain.

"Do they drink it?" Clover said as he returned, handing him a kitchen towel.

"Don't know," he said. "Myself, I'm of the opinion that they don't eat nothin' we eat. But it's rude not to put it out, and rudeness ain't our way."

She gave him a look that suggested that he could not possibly believe that discourtesy might be humanity's greatest offense, and he must *surely* have intended to discuss the dire consequences of failing to display appropriate respect, or rather, the combined terror and gratitude due to those who protected the grass and the grain, and the loss of whose favour meant that no one dared speak of the victims, nor drive past their blasted lands. But an adult's shorthand to save time or face was nothing new to her, and she nodded, while Marla came downstairs to fuss over her filthy clothing and soaked hair.

...

The summons came in late June, while Arnold was out patching a tractor tire, a painstaking job which brooked no shortcuts, and so it was the absence of sound that alerted him to the presence of the gods—the neighbour's boys playing on the asphalt pad behind the quonset fell silent, the crack of the basketball dribbling into nothingness; the cows cut themselves off mid-low; birds raced for the sparse trees.

Arnold looked up from the tire, and there they were: great translucent bodies pushing through the wheat and barley, a green-gold sea parting, heading for the house. He was up and running before he even realized what he was doing, before his knees informed him it was a bad idea, leaving black epoxy fingerprints on the back door.

Marla and Clover were staring at the summons between them, bright on the worn wood of the kitchen table—a green nest, woven grass and sagebrush, a little coil of fragrance and innocence, holding in its depths something darkly glowing. At the sink, Mrs. Collier from down the road stood openmouthed, still holding the mug she'd been rinsing. Marla's tea had spilled onto her placemat, turning the pale pink blood-red. After a moment, Mrs. Collier quavered, "Well! A personal visit from Those of the Hills and the Green! What a *lucky* girl!"

And Marla, too, rallied, and their voices rose in pitch as they discussed outfits, whether her patent-leather Christmas shoes might still fit, appropriate jewelry, and Arnold stared at the child and thought about what knife would do, and who to call in town these days to get a spot in the special cemetery, because they needed a while to set up the signs and dig the. . .

She was watching him, he realized, waiting for his reaction, and he'd trained her for that, of course, trained her for dogs and bears and coyotes and bulls—you don't move first. You wait to see what they do, and then you move. They move, and then you move. He exhaled slowly, and said, "Well, lemme just wash my hands, and we can talk about dinner."

"I can pick anything, right?" Clover said; her voice was brassy and distant with shock, a darkness already settling over her, gray over the bright eyes.

"Anything you want," he said.

They decided on spaghetti and meatballs in Grandma's secret sauce, and Arnold went back out to finish his patching job, and the boys took their basketball and went home, and after a few hours, the cattle unbunched from their knot and began to graze again.

A summons was not a request, of course, not a true request to which anyone might reply that they were unavailable, or that it was too far; a request implied that refusal was an option, and it was not. Their only grace lay in knowing that it was not. Indeed, it was a sovereign honour, being summoned, deemed not only adequate but desired by the only beings that were permitted to judge such things. Arnold told himself that a thousand times for the next eight days, watching the child run amongst the calves and weed the garden and nap with the dogs and sort her dolls to see which one she might allow to be buried with her.

On the eighth morning, Arnold woke to find Marla up and rummaging in the closet, knocking over boxes and bags. In the hallway a dog's nails clicked, someone curious about the noise. "No," he said, unnecessarily. "You already know you can't."

"Like hell I can't," she hissed, not turning. She unearthed the suitcase, like many of their nicer things left by one of the older girls, and stepped over the piles of clothing, heading for Clover's room.

Arnold managed to grab her just before she reached the scribbled and stickered door. "You know that's never worked," he said.

"There's a first time for everything."

"Yeah, and I bet they all said that, when they tried." He pulled at the suitcase. She locked both hands onto it and glared at him in the thin light creeping into the hallway.

"We've got till sundown. Technically. If I—"

"No."

"*Technically*. If I can just get her to—"

"You know what happens."

"Fight me on this, Arnold," she said. "For once in your goddamned life!"

But he fell silent, and his hand fell away from the suitcase, and after a moment she flung the thing at his feet and began to sob, backing away so that the sleeping girl would not hear.

Clover wanted to change before dinner, but Marla put her foot down: Did she really want to present herself splattered with tomato sauce? So she ate in her pajamas, and slurped and sprayed as much sauce as she liked.

"Was this one of our cows?" Clover asked, forking up a meatball.

"Yes. A boy cow," Arnold said. "A steer. Could probably find his number, you want."

"Good," she said.

"Good?"

"Well, if it's ours, then it should be ours forever," she said vaguely, waving her fork, then replacing the meatball and finishing her pasta.

Afterwards, teeth brushed, hair curled, scented with Mr. Bubbles and a dab of Barbie perfume, she was allowed to put on the blue silk dress and the slightly-too-tight Christmas shoes, and the three of them stood on the porch for a few minutes in the long, low summer light. Shortest night of the year, Arnold almost said, then thought better of it. His daughter's night would have no end.

"I'll take her," Arnold said under his breath.

"But it's. . . " Marla began, and hesitated; in truth there was no rule that a mother must take a daughter, a father a son. And to be there at the last moment. . . How to live with that? Of course it could be done, had been done since time immemorial. But how, how? She couldn't imagine. "Well, take the new truck, at least."

Kissed, blessed, face wiped, ribbons adjusted, Clover finally left her mother on the porch and let Arnold lift her into the truck, so that her dress wouldn't get dusty. He put the velvet-lined box containing his best chef's knife on her lap, watched her fingers curl protectively around it. Got too attached to things, he thought. Loved too much. Maybe not been loved enough. The way it works out here. "Hold onto that," he said. "Don't let it bump around. Ruins the edge."

"I won't."

It would have been a long walk out to the gods; he watched their wide, shivering bodies approach in the darkness as he drove. They set a sedate pace on the gravel road till it ran out, and he continued into the pasture, the smell of sage rising through the vents. Far above, clouds parted around the waiting crowd, their tapering bodies a star-filled blackness fading into the twilight, violet and lilac where they met the grass. The wind delivered the odour of rotting things, compost, crumbling old manure, overlaid with the high reek of ozone. Clover coughed, curled around the box.

He stopped a hundred yards from the altar, thrown up, as always, by unseen hands, just a few thick slabs of sod so hastily assembled that in the darkness it looked like a haystack. His heart was hammering, skipping beats. Too old for this, he thought. Too old to have had her in the first place. Our mistake. Mine.

"Are we walking the rest of the way?" Clover said.

He glanced at her, the stone of the summons still shining faintly through the pocket of her dress. "Out you get," he said, and came around the truck to help her onto the running board.

His worn plaid shirt reached her shins, but she looked like she always did, forever digging up and wearing her brothers' old clothes. He passed his belt through the sleeves of her dress and buckled it back on, the silk so thin he didn't even have to move up a hole. "Gimme your hand a second, and hold your breath," he said.

She nodded, and only faintly whimpered as he passed the knife over her palm. He took her hand and pressed blood onto the silk dress, his t-shirt, even his beard, her cool fingers brushing his eyelids. When he was done, she picked up the summons balanced on the bumper and blinked uncertainly. He knew what she wanted to say, what no one needed to say: It stayed with the honoree. No one else dared even touch it. Blasphemy's reward was not merely immediate death, but lands blighted for a dozen lifetimes over.

But though it burned and squirmed in his dry palm, he lived: the final test passed. In the far darkness, the chanting had begun. He must reach the altar before it ended, or the deception would be worthless. There was time enough for one last kiss, carefully placed on her forehead, the way she kissed the dogs, and one last piece of advice: "Wrap that hand up," he said. "There's clean hankies in the glove compartment. Stay inside the truck until your mama comes to get you. There's coyotes out there."

"I'm not afraid of coyotes," she said, and the tears finally came, running from eyes and nose. She wiped her face on her plaid sleeve.

"I know you're not," he said. He handed her the truck keys before he walked away, the dress billowing behind him, knife in his hand, towards the altar of the gods, their willing sacrifice willingly come.

###

About the Author

Premee Mohamed is a scientist and spec fic writer working out of Canada. Her work has appeared in *Syntax and Salt, Metaphorosis,* Alliteration Ink's *No Sh!t, There I Was* anthology, Innsmouth Free Press's 2016 World Fantasy Award-winning *She Walks In Shadows* anthology, the *Molotov Cocktail*, and others. Look for her upcoming work in *Nightmare Magazine* and *Far Fetched Fables.*

*****~~~~~*****

The Great Man's Iron Horse

by Mark Mellon

"Come one, come all. Only a sluggard poltroon would miss such a golden opportunity for simultaneous education and excitement. Don't be a lollygag or a mollycoddle. Gather around instead to see the greatest engineering marvel since early man built the Pyramids."

The foghorn voice carried loud and clear over the din from a four-piece orchestra, awkward but spirited, a strange, exotic polka on trumpet, oboe, accordion, and kettle drum. Denizens of Dewlap Junction emerged from sod shanties and wooden shacks and flocked to the edge of town to witness the spectacle, all one hundred fifty of them. A one-dog town with no distinction other than being the terminus of a bankrupt railroad, it was a great day in the morning in western Kansas, the middle of nowhere, almost as good as the circus come to town.

"Don't be shy. Don't be bashful. Step up, ladies and gentlemen, why, even children, to see the modern miracle of American industrial prowess. Conceived by my own Olympian brain, that of Eufimus T. Broadsnatch, if I may put false modesty aside."

The portly man who strode the wooden stage wore a bright yellow frock coat with a daisy in the boutonniere, a plaid waistcoat, and red-and-white striped trousers. His eighteen-inch stovepipe hat towered over his red face, graced by a prominent nose, the mark of all eminent men.

He was a striking figure, but not in the least the reason for the rubes' fascination. What drew open mouthed gawks and stares was the shrouded figure that towered behind the stage, draped in sacking, split and sewn together.

A man in a buff beaverskin plug hat and a jade green cutaway lurked at the crowd's edge. He beckoned a nearby snot-nosed street urchin to approach. Suspicious, but intrigued, the stunted runt complied.

"Kid, how'd you like two bits?"

"Doing what, bub?"

"Razz that fat man. Whatever he sells, pour cold water on it."

Face half hidden by a canted, broad brimmed cap, the punk sneered.

"Easier than killing chickens. Only where's the scratch?"

"Just give Broadsnatch the bird, and you'll get paid sure. Ask for Jonah Carriot at the Union Atlantic office. I'm manager there."

"I don't care if you're President, Mister. Either fork over two bits, or I catch laryngitis."

"Well, all right, if you're going to be difficult," Carriot grumbled.

He handed the kid a quarter. The kid bit on it, slipped it into a pocket, and pushed to the front.

"For months, I and my Bohemian minions have labored in the wilderness, secluded from human society and its luxuries, sworn to secrecy, dedicated solely to our endeavor, with no other comfort provided to me than the company of my exquisite young daughter, Penny Bright Broadsnatch."

He bowed to the willowy young blonde at the stage's edge. The top hat fell from his head, tumbled down his outstretched arm, and into his waiting hand. Broadsnatch replaced his hat as his daughter curtsied to the crowd to applause, the loudest from a handsome young man in Eastern attire. The kid stuck out his tongue and blew a loud raspberry. Broadsnatch scowled and scanned the crowd, but was unable to see the kid due to his diminutive status.

"As I was saying, I, Broadsnatch, engineer, entrepreneur, and inventor extraordinaire, will now present my brainchild to my scientific peers, an expectant general public, and the entire world from crowned heads of Europe to the heathen Chinee."

The kid piped up. "Oh, apple sauce. Just what are you talking about anyway, Mister? Why don't you make sense for a change?"

"Go away, kid. You bother me. Ladies and gentlemen, is the fourth estate represented among you?"

"That'd be me, Calvin Suggs," a cadaver in a faded black suit and broad brimmed Quaker hat said. "Editor and reporter for the *Dewlap Weekly Blatt*. Course I'm blacksmith, undertaker, and justice of the peace too, take your pick. Since you asked me to put my press hat on, what on earth you got under that there sacking? Reckon we got a right to know what you been up to, Broadsnatch."

"Suggs ain't whistling '*Dixie*,'" an old crow in a poke bonnet said. "We ain't had a decent night's sleep for months since you showed up with them dern foreigners and commenced that godawful racket. What sort of monstrosity you hiding there, Broadsnatch?"

"Suffering sciatica, Madam. How you talk. As if any product of science could be monstrous."

"He ain't got nothing. He's just the bunk," the kid said.

"I told you to beat it, kid. Let me end this ignorant, foozling speculation forthwith. Alois, Janos, Milos, Emaus. The ropes."

The tall, husky men set their musical instruments aside and ran to long cords that dangled from the shroud's edges. They tugged the covering away. To the crowd's open-mouthed amazement, a huge horse was revealed, not some crude, Trojan contraption lashed together from driftwood, but a modern, industrial steed, a steel stallion, one hundred fifty hands high. Jointed machinery surmounted the front and hind quarters, each powered by a steam engine. A railroad car comprised the torso. Two glass windows were set in the horse's eyes with the engineer's compartment in the head.

"Behold the greatest wonder of the nineteenth century. A giant equinomotive. While Eastern captains of industry waste time, money, and men trying to build a transcontinental railroad, I have sliced the Gordian knot with characteristic ease. My steam-powered horse can cross plain and desert, surmount any mountaintop or rugged range, ford any river, with no need for tracks, independent and alone, able to take any course almost at whim. I propose to demonstrate the truth of those asseverations on the morrow by the one means that no man can gainsay, that of action. Come the dawn, I and my brave Bohemian black gang shall strike westward with San Francisco as our ultimate goal. Not only that, I shall make the trip in three days, more than five hundred miles a day."

The kid laughed long and hard. "Ah, banana oil."

Broadsnatch pointed behind the crowd, eyes wide as though with wonder.

"Godfrey Daniel, look at the plumage on that extraordinary bird."

Everyone turned to see, including the kid. Broadsnatch took a pebble from a coat pocket and slung it with unerring accuracy. The stone hit the kid in the back of the head. He ran, hands to his head, tears streaming as he screamed.

"Told you to scram, you little cheeseworm," Broadsnatch muttered.

"Folks, tomorrow we leave for San Francisco. And any among you who wishes to take the journey of a lifetime may come along and enjoy every luxury in the

Broadsnatch Express wagon-lit, fine as anything on the East Coast or the Continent, all for the modest sum of a hundred dollars in gold. Yes, that's right, dear friends, a mere five double eagles lets you make history while living like a king. Who could resist such an invitation? Don't press too hard, folks. Happy to accommodate you one at a time."

No one approached. Women in worn, sack dresses and poke bonnets, men in ragged homespun and battered hats, stared at him coldly, indifferently, each face a study in blank indifference.

"What? You mean to say there's no person of spirit among you who still breathes the heady air of the Conquistadors and seeks new worlds to conquer? Not a one of you doesn't want to ride my iron horse to Frisco Bay?"

"You're right welcome to head there yourself, Broadsnatch," Suggs said. "And I hope you and your horse tromp right into the Bay and drown."

Broadsnatch's face grew redder. He raised his rattan cane as if ready to strike Suggs. His daughter was about to intervene when a voice rang out, female but brassy, loud as a Civil War heavy mortar.

"Me and my son will ride that contraption if you can reach San Fransisky quick as you say."

A short woman in black widow's weeds with a red carpetbag stood in the crowd, by her side a young, thin blond man, velvet suit creased and dusty from travel. Broadsnatch beamed.

"Ah, a woman with that true frontier spunk. Who might you be, Madam?"

"Mabel Stump, of the Galena Stumps. This is my son, Clarence."

"A fine young scion too. That will be two hundred U.S. dollars for you both."

"What makes you so all fired anxious to get halfway across the country, widder?" Suggs asked.

"Please, sir, mind your own business," Clarence said.

"Oh, hush, Clarence," Mabel said. "I'll tell you straight, Suggs. I'm going to shoot my husband, Ted Stump. He ditched me and Clarence in '49 to pan gold. If the rotten old fool stayed, he'd have cashed in when they struck lead in the back forty acres. I used the money to live in style and put Clarence through Harvard. Now he's grown, I'm going to show him what happens to rotten skunks what don't honor their marriage vows. I ain't no widow yet, but I'm going to be soon enough."

"An admirable sentiment, Mrs. Stump," Broadsnatch said. "Is there anyone else ready to embark upon this heroic journey?"

"I'll go," the young man in front shouted. "It sounds like a real lark. Put down Marlowe P. Rodgin for your best berth."

"The right spirit, my collegiate friend. I'll reserve our finest tick mattress with a slight surcharge of fifty dollars."

"I'll take it, happily."

"Spoken like a gentleman. Now we have three bold travelers. Surely there must be at least one more with an itch to ramble?"

A hulking man clad in black stepped forth. Features obscured by a broad brimmed hat and a scarf swathed about his face, he was a macabre figure.

"I'll go," he croaked.

Even Broadsnatch was momentarily daunted by his funereal mien.

"Ah, yes, just so. And your name, sir?"

"Does it matter? Ain't my money good enough?"

"Of course it is. And so, ladies and gentlemen, with passengers and cargo aboard, we shall take our leave of you with the horizon's first crimsoning."

"Tain't soon enough if you ask me," the crone said. "Good riddance to bad rubbish."

Broadsnatch tipped his hat.

"And I bid you good day also, Madam." He muttered, "Hope you fall in the creek and drown going home, you old biddy."

...

The Tinhorn Saloon was the only dive in town, a big tent with a kerosene lantern hung from the tentpole, cheap tables and chairs, and a bar made from two barrels and a door. They served flat beer and redeye. Broadsnatch held forth before the local yokels, Suggs among them.

"It was in my mountain man days back during the savage winter of '50. I'd slain a bear and was dragging him back to my lean-to so I could butcher him properly."

"You dragged a bear alone? Even if it was a cub, that sounds like a stretcher," Suggs said.

"I was considerably stronger in those days due to my outdoor regimen. When only a few miles from my crude shelter, I was suddenly set upon by my most bitter enemies, Blackfeet warriors. They loosed a volley of arrows at me, but with my usual presence of mind, I shielded myself with the bear. There were too many to take on alone, so I leaped off a nearby precipice into a swift running river."

"In the dead of winter? Sounds like you'd most froze to death. Don't know if I buy that one either, Broadsnatch."

"I insulated myself with the bear's carcass. At last, shaken from my ordeal, I washed up on the riverbank. I rose only to see my hated enemies before me, eyes lit with bloodlust. Without hesitation, I cast the bear aside, drew my butcher knife, and cut my way through a wall of living human flesh."

"If they had bows and arrows, why didn't they just shoot you?"

"I was too quick for them. I returned at last to my lean-to and prepared a bear stew."

"The bear you threw aside?"

"He was delicious with mustard."

Nearby, Carriot sat at a table with an ill-favored man with a perpetual toothy leer.

"That's the one I want taken care of."

Dick Weed sniggered.

"If you want to stop that iron horse, why can't me and the boys take some coal oil and torch it?"

Carriot shook his head.

"Those Bohocks keep watch with shotguns. Broadsnatch is an easy target. Call him out, then shoot him down. There's five thousand in it. This way you don't have to split it."

Weed shook his head and sniggered again.

"He ain't armed. Folks'll lynch me."

"Not if you ride out afterward."

"You might could have a point. What's he done anyway to get you so mad?"

"I'll tell you if you quit giggling like an idiot. Broadsnatch is a menace to the railroad industry. If he can prove that iron horse works, the Union Atlantic is ruined. I'll do anything to see that doesn't happen."

"Consider her done, son."

Weed slouched over to Broadsnatch.

"Mister, you're the biggest damn liar I ever saw. What do you think of them apples?"

Broadsnatch drew away, fear plain in his eyes.

"Why, sir, how dare you impugn my integrity? Would a man of such accomplishment as myself, a holder of degrees from the finest universities in America and Europe, even need to stoop to low aggrandizement?"

Weed sniggered. "I didn't understand a damn word you said, and I still know you're lying. I hate a liar worse than anything. I'll take care of you like the others."

He reached down for his pistol. A shot rang out. The bullet barely missed Weed's face. Startled, terrified, he turned to face Mabel Stump. Wisps of smoke trailed from the .45 Navy Colt in her left hand.

"I'll put the next one through you, you bastard."

"You ain't got no call to interfere in a man's quarrel, lady," Weed said.

"And furthermore, women ain't allowed here. This is a respectable place," the bartender added.

"Shut up, both of you. This pistol makes me more man than either of you. You sidle on out like the snake you are. I ain't fooling."

Stump had Weed dead to rights, and he knew it. He crawfished, holstered his pistol, and slunk from the saloon to jeers and boos.

"A coward at heart like every bully. Madame Stump, I'm forever indebted to you."

"Broadsnatch, ain't nothing standing between me and Callyforny. You get back to camp. You'll need sleep if we leave at dawn."

Broadsnatch looked longingly at the redeye on the bar. He was about to speak when Mabel waved her pistol barrel toward the tent flap. He tipped his hat.

"I bow to inevitable fate."

He left, followed by Mabel.

...

"Well, Weed, for such a big, bad outlaw, that old prune sure made you cry calf rope."

The two men spoke in hushed whispers, hidden in the livery stable.

"You shut your mouth, Carriot. What could I do with her shading me? I'll fix her and that blowhard Broadsnatch too. Me and my gang will riddle them with holes, them and that dern iron horse."

"That's more like it. Remember, there's five thousand if you do. But how will you catch him if that iron horse goes as fast as Broadsnatch claims?"

"Don't you worry none, hoss. I'll ride out tonight with my gang, get a head start. They have to go through Chagrin Gulch. We'll ambush 'em there dressed up as Indians so we don't get blamed."

"That Stump woman's a crack shot. What if she cuts up rough?"

"I got an inside man on this job, Carriot. We'll get 'er done."

. . .

Baleful, red rays at dawn pierced Broadsnatch's eyes and ended his stupor. He looked disconsolately about him at a pain-filled landscape and almost fell from the hammock doing so.

"Eh, what happened? The Confederate Army must have retreated over me last night."

"You drank too much, that's what," Mabel said, already up and dressed. "Ted was a soak too, probably still is, at least until I finish him. I'll have Clarence fetch water."

Broadsnatch grimaced. "Never touch the stuff."

"Don't be silly," Penny said. "Father always has his pick me up in the morning. It sets him right as rain."

She handed him a tumbler full of a fizzing white liquid and propped him up to drink it.

"What's in that stuff?"

"A secret formula, Mrs. Stump. A homeopathic cure of my own devising."

"Smells like more alcohol to me."

"Only a minute amount for medicinal purposes."

Broadsnatch knocked back the potion. A huge, volcanic belch erupted from his mouth. Instantly, he was out of the hammock and on his feet.

"Alois, hot water and my razor. Emaus, lay out my captain's uniform in the tent. Milos, Janos, fetch the passengers and their traps. We leave on the nonce."

The crew went efficiently about their tasks. The passengers climbed into a large basket held by sturdy chains and were winched up into the car. Engines were fired and boilers stoked. Twin, thick columns of black smoke poured skyward. Broadsnatch emerged, resplendent in blue and gold, captain's cap jauntily angled.

He puffed a cigar. With surprising agility for a man of his girth and age, he nimbly clambered up handholds in the right front leg to the neck, where he entered through a hatch and went up an interior ladder to the engineer's chair in the head. Broadsnatch sat in the padded leather chair. He shouted into the speaking horns.

"Passengers safely belayed? Steam up in both boilers? Answer me, you Bohemian bunglers."

"*Ano pane*, yes, sir," four voices shouted.

"Then we're off."

He grabbed a long lever, pulled the hand release, advanced it, and did the same for the lever's mate. Slowly, ponderously at first, and then more rapidly, the horse's elaborate gears and pistons pumped and pushed, turned and interlinked. Long, jointed legs lifted massive hooves. They moved with increasing speed and confidence. The horse walked westward. The crew stoked the fires on the boilers' open platforms, each man tethered to a railing by a rope around his waist in the event of a fall. The sun fully crested the low, flat horizon and clad the iron horse in gold. Dewlap Junctioneers gaped and cheered as the horse slowly clomped away.

"Well, I'll be derned. It works after all," Suggs said.

"Ah, it'll fall apart before they go five miles," the kid said.

"One way or another, Broadsnatch will never reach San Francisco," Carriot said.

...

Several miles from town, alone on the broad prairie, Broadsnatch shouted into the speaker horns.

"Milos, Alois. Bring the boilers to double pressure. Trotting speed."

"*Ano pane*."

They threw wood into the boilers to build more heat and pressure. Smoke plumes shot high, black lines in the blue. The horse moved into a steady trot. As with a real horse, the legs moved in rhythm, left front in time with the right rear and vice versa. Two governors controlled their motion, diagonal, jointed rods over the railroad car that synchronously pushed and pulled. Fifteen-yard legs devoured the ground at frightening speed. Landscape flashed by, offering glimpses through the eye portholes of undulating brown steppe, vast skies, flocks of birds, and buffalo herds in wild, panicked retreat from the oncoming iron monster. Broadsnatch looked on stolidly as he vigorously puffed his cigar. Periodically, he sipped from a large flask in his coat pocket. He steered by slight delays of speed on the left or right levers that caused the horse to veer as needed.

The horse may have moved swiftly, but not comfortably. Passengers tumbled about violently. Though they were lashed to their seats with thick cushions, every hoof fall still slammed them hard. Trapped, they had no choice but to endure as the journey's early steps threatened to grind their vertebrae into dust.

"This is such amazing fun. You must be proud to have a father who's a brilliant inventor," Rodgin said to Penny.

She looked away.

"Well, there's nothing pretentious about Father."

"He's got much to be proud of. Look what a nice daughter he has."

"I must say, you're very fresh."

Rodgin smiled charmingly.

"We're going to get acquainted sooner or later, confined as we are. Might as well start."

"Be quiet, squirt," the man in black said. "It's hard enough sitting here while my brains get pounded and also hear you spout mush. Just put a sock in it, will you?"

"Say, I don't have to take that. I'm an educated man from a good family. Why, I bet you don't even have one."

The stranger snarled and reached to untie the ropes that held him. There was the unmistakable click of a hammer being pulled back on a single action pistol. Mabel sat by Clarence, Colt in hand.

"I need this trip peaceable so it's quicker. I don't want anyone kicking up a fuss. Quarrel or spoon as you like, but after we see that blue bay water. Understand?"

There was no resisting that sinister glare. Both men hung their heads submissively.

"That's better. Downright neighborly."

She replaced the Colt in the carpetbag.

The great iron horse came to low, red brown hills. A pass led through them, Chagrin Gulch. Broadsnatch headed his creation toward the narrow defile.

"This looks tricky. Slow to a walk, boys."

The crew reduced boiler pressure. The horse slowed to a more easily endured walk. The gulch's narrow flanks were just above the horse's head. Broadsnatch steered carefully, placed one hoof after another through the winding, narrow defile. He kept a wary eye out.

"It's quiet. Maybe too quiet."

...

Hungry and tired after a long night's ride, Weed and his men sat their horses, dressed in buckskins, made up in black wigs, feathers, and war paint. Alerted by the smoke plumes, they stood atop a hill above the pass.

"Now, when that contraption's right underneath, we ride down hell for leather, whooping and hollering like Kiowa, hold up the iron horse, plug 'em, and ride out, easy as pie."

"How do we stop a fifty-foot-tall iron horse?" one man said.

"Kid Galoot's my inside man. You'll see."

"Sounds risky," another said.

"Shut up and do as I say." Weed sniggered to re-assert his authority.

The ground lurched and shook, stirred by the heavy hooves' approaching thud.

"Here she comes. Get ready."

...

The horse came to a sharp hairpin turn.

"I need fortification," Broadsnatch said.

He reached for his flask. Wild screams and war whoops interrupted him. Pistol shots rang out. Through the left porthole, he glimpsed horsemen at the gallop down a hill's slope, brandishing firearms.

"Shadrach, Mesach, and Abednego. Savages. We're under attack. Janos *et alia*, protect yourselves."

Exposed in the open, the crew took shelter behind the boilers. Without a steady input of fuel, the engines lost pressure. The great iron horse slowed. Mabel untied her ropes and went to a window to investigate. A bullet smashed through the glass, passing inches from her head.

"Marauders."

She reached into her carpetbag for the Colt.

"Hold it, biddy. I got you covered."

The man in black's derringer pointed at Mabel. She scowled, but pulled her hand from the carpetbag.

"I had you down for a bad actor."

"I'm a better man than you'll ever be. I'm Kid Galoot, and that's my gang out there."

"Huh. Not even real Indians. I can't abide a fraud."

"Regardless, you'll keep still till this holdup's done."

A fist shot out and caught Kid Galoot square on the chin, a knockout blow. The Kid fell, unconscious. Rodgin stood over him, rubbing his knuckles. Penny came to him and caressed his hand.

"That was so brave."

"Three years in the Harvard Boxing Club came in handy."

"Thanks for the assist. Now I can fix those bandits," Mabel said, snaking out her pistol. She smashed out a window's glass, cocked the pistol, took careful aim, and fired. A bandit screamed and fell from his horse. Startled by unexpected opposition, the other riders scattered. Free from harassing fire, the crew resumed their posts, and heaved wood into the boilers. Engines regained pressure; hooves moved with new vigor.

"Alois. Milos. Tromping mode."

The two rearmost men slammed on brakes, massive, circular brass affairs with asbestos pads, another Broadsnatch innovation. The horse halted and reared up on his hind legs. Everyone in the railroad car slid precipitously to the back. Forelegs wildly flailed in the air.

"Hightail it, boys, or we're pressed ham," an outlaw screamed.

"You won't escape, you wretched miscreants," Broadsnatch shouted.

Iron hooves descended with deadly force. Terrified by the monstrous apparition, the real horses boogered, threw their riders, and fled. Weed lay on his back, the wind knocked from him. He looked up to see the enormous circular outline of a black hoof overhead and had time for one last snigger before he was squashed flat as a bug. The remaining bandits fled for their lives.

Shortly afterward, the great horse passed from Chagrin Gulch to broad plains again. In the far distance, the Rockies' purple peaks loomed. Broadsnatch once again raised the pace to a ground-devouring trot. Penny joined him, seating herself in the spot next to his.

"Greetings, daughter. How fare the passengers?"

"Oh, well enough I suppose, Pops. We got Kid Galoot trussed up good and tight. Mabel's watching him. And—"

"Yes, Penny, my dear. There's something else, isn't there? Something important."

Penny blushed and looked downward.

"I've met a fellow I like. Marlie Rodgin."

"Ah, the Ivy Leaguer."

"I first thought he was forward and stuck up, but it turns out he's very brave and modest about it too. Father, I need to know. Do you approve of him?"

"If his social connections are sound and his father proves amenable to an occasional soft touch, why, of course, daughter."

Penny clapped her hands together in joy.

"Father, you've made me so happy. But there's something wrong here. I'm sitting on something."

"Nonsense, my dear."

"No, I am. And I can hear squeaking."

Penny got out of the seat, released the catch, and lifted it back. Under the seat huddled a group of tiny, newborn, pink mice, squealing and hungry.

"Oh, how curious. I wonder what their parents were."

"Careless, my dear. Careless."

And so, Broadsnatch's iron horse thundered on across the untracked wilderness, its confident albeit well lubricated inventor at the helm and Manifest Destiny his destination, another potent herald of inevitable American progress and civilization.

###

About the Author

Mark Mellon is a novelist who supports his family by working as an attorney. His short fiction recently appeared in *Deadman's Tome, Yellow Mama,* and *Thuglit.* He's published four novels and over fifty short stories in the USA, UK, and Ireland. A novella, *Escape From Byzantium*, won the 2010 Independent Publisher Silver Medal for fantasy and science fiction. Mark's website is www.mellonwritesagain.com.

*****~~~~~*****

The Hunt

by Salinda Tyson

The Grandmother breathed out slowly, squeezing a drop of blood from her finger onto the ground, summoning and shaping her Servant, whirling across the prairie, slamming together tumbleweeds and shed snakeskins and earth to form horse and rider.

She who served the Grandmother rode fast and furious. Her spirit horse was made of mesquite bark, spines of saguaro, tumbleweeds, dust devils, rattlesnake skins, and the warm south wind. It skimmed the tall prairie grass, the plains, the mesas and arroyos. The Servant rode bareback, her black and white and sage-green hair streaming behind her like a great serpent rushing through the air.

Once human herself, the Servant now served the balance of the human and the natural. Her bones, her hair, her soul, and that of her steed knew, because they were joined in a vast awareness that held time like a toy, that their passage carried them over the dried-up seas of an ancient time, where great flesh-eating lizards had roamed the lush jungles and fern-forests. The great blood-lusty predators and kin had gobbled many species of smaller, milder temperament, who did nothing more violent than rip aquatic plants from marsh bottoms. But when catastrophe darkened the earth, cutting the vast plant supplies the vegetarian lizards lived on, they and the predators had died out, starving in agony, a slow, merciless death in a drying and cooling time. And the rat-like mammals that climbed the evolutionary tree to turn into monkeys and primates at last became human, coming to dominate all other lands and beings.

Perhaps it was the fact of rats and rat nature forming the base of the tall ancient family tree that had allowed such conniving meanness to seep into and harden in the hearts of humankind.

She shook her head. Heat lightning flicked jagged spears across the sky. Thunder rumbled. The Grandmother's Servant tossed her train of writhing rattlesnake hair, bent over her steed's neck, and rode the wind.

...

The Kansas Pacific train rocked and swayed on the steel tracks. Its steam whistle screamed. The great metal wheels slowed as the engineer began braking the engine. Scent of hot metal filled the air. Eager hunters had already opened the windows that looked north along the tracks. They propped their hunting rifles out the windows, sighting along the sleek expensive barrels, adjusting sights, firing to test how the wind would affect accuracy. They licked their lips in anticipation.

The herd of buffalo or bison would soon come in sight.

The engineer and conductor had promised good sport. Scouts habitually rode the plains along the railroad tracks, reporting herds and their direction of travel at the nearest telegraph office. Sometimes, on their employers' orders, they drove the bison nearer the path of the train. Especially if one of the big bosses was on board and eager for "sport."

...

In a car with her female companions, Lydia Mae Brinkman stroked her gloved hand over the stock of her

Springfield single-shot rifle, moved down the aisle, and chose a window. She was a very good shot, a dead-eye, and had privately bet she could outdo the men on the train.

Ladies, known as "Dianas" to the gents on the train, customarily claimed the meat of the hunt. Where would the buffalo meat go? That was no one's business but hers.

"Hunting dead ahead," the conductor yelled as he swayed down the aisle. "Gentlemen, ladies, ready your rifles."

Frank McCray had bet he would down the first shaggy hump. Fifty gold dollars on the first kill.

He had also bet on how many kills could be made in five minutes. Low wager was twenty, high wager, 90. The natives depended on the bison for food, but frankly he did not care. Dead buffalo dotting the plains would mean more meat for the pitiful tribes to scavenge, he thought. If scores were killed, could the Indians butcher them fast enough? Or would they simply draw flies, coyotes, wolves, and vultures to pick the carcasses down to bone and break down the great bodies beneath the incredible blue sky.

His friend Randall Stevens balanced atop a car, braced against a rigged blind on the roof, his hair ruffled by the breeze. He sought challenge, to make a hunt as difficult as possible. "Give-the-beast-a-chance Stevens," the other sportsmen called him. The wind had snatched his hat away. McCray whooped and put a bullet dead center through the crown of that hat, which had spun away as the locomotive snaked on across the plain.

The train ran parallel to the herds that were heading south for their winter grazing grounds. Behind the thrum of the locomotive, Frank swore he felt the earth trembling. Bison herds moved in clustered thousands.

A sudden stench rushed into the windows of the compartments. Excited cries came from the passengers; fingers pointed. Several dead bulls, their noses in the dirt, with crows and vultures squawking and pecking, jockeying for position on their bodies, lay beyond the tracks. Some had been cleaned to the bone. An Indian family, a horseman, a woman and a child, was hurriedly butchering a distant beast, salvaging what they could, dragging it away on a travois. The man waved his arm at a vulture. The scavenger settled in the dry grass near a dead bull bison, its wattled, naked neck drawn into its shoulder blades, ugly beak and head bent forward, bidding its time. It shifted from foot to foot, impatient to tear into flesh and gorge.

A crow screamed and flew at the train window, perhaps attacking its own reflection in the rushing glass. It shrieked again and flew upward, skimming Stevens's blind. Startled, he jerked upright and almost lost his balance. The crow perched on the blind, and stared him down. It opened that sharp beak and made a sound like a harsh laugh. Not a crow, a raven, Stevens saw, a huge one. Rough feathering under the beak and an eerie intelligence in the bright black eyes. Stevens steadied himself with his rifle butt against the roof of the car. Ravens had worked over the battlefields he had survived when he carried a rifle for the Union Army, the Grand Army of the Republic. It must have been drawn to the dead bison, he thought. He cursed the bird, spread his legs farther apart for better balance. It eyed him, let out a raucous caw, and flew off, squirting guano over the blind.

Stevens laughed. Damn birds. But he'd seen himself reflected in its eye.

That bothered him, the way a thing struck him as an omen.

...

The Servant lowered her metal and leather and glass goggles from her helmet, to protect her eyes and face against the sparks and iron shavings the metal wheels threw up. She rode alongside the train, keening a song of life and death, gathering the souls of the bison and the creatures who lived on them and cleaned their bones, deep into her all-encompassing spirit. Ravens flew in her wake, settled on her saguaro needle shoulders, whispered in her right ear and her left ear the number of hunters, the size of the herds ahead. Report given, they launched themselves and winged ahead.

In her bones of earth and air, water and fire, she saw the heart of the man atop the train. *The one whose heart could be changed.* She snatched a bow from the ether, nocked an arrow forged from a spark of lightning, and shot it straight into his chest.

. . .

Stevens was knocked to his knees. *My heart?* He gasped for breath. A great weight pressed outward against his ribs. My god, he thought. Tears burned his eyes. He stared at his hand gripping the well-cared-for Enfield rifle, the old weapon that he had cleaned and oiled so many times, carried across deadly wheat fields and into muddy, hopeless trenches. His hands shook. Bile rushed into his mouth. He flattened himself on the car's roof, praying he would live.

And he knew he wasn't going to shoot buffalo or anything, not today or tomorrow or day after tomorrow.

No matter what McCray and the other men or ladies did or said.

. . .

The Servant leaped aboard the train, flinging her body through an open window, sliding over Lydia's rifle, which was pointed out a window.

Women hunting, women killing. The Servant spat in fury. The rattlesnakes in her hair coiled and shook their tails. She lowered her goggles. Her eyes blazed.

The rifle's owner fell backward into the aisle. "Who the devil are you?" she demanded. Her eyes fixed on the snakes. Her lady companions stared spellbound.

"One who asks you," the intruder said, "to stop killing, to give the meat to those on the reservation."

"You have no right to ask me anything. Leave this car, or I shall scream for assistance." Lydia grabbed her rifle, which smelled of gunpowder, broke it open, and thrust in a bullet."I warn you."

The stranger sighed. In her hair the snakes rose. Their rattles vibrated so fast they buzzed. Their heads and tongues darted back and forth.

"Sister." The stranger laughed and put her hand on Lydia's chest. The hand sunk into Lydia's flesh, until it rested against her heart. Lydia gasped and fainted.

The Servant touched many more. Some died, their hearts stopped. Minutes later, men and women, hunters all, now stared from the windows in awe and shock, watching in wonder as the great herd grazed. A party had left the train to butcher downed bison and carry the meat to the baggage car. They resumed their seats with shamed faces. Rifles had been unloaded, gathered, and propped against the walls, along with ammunition boxes.

The conductor walked the aisles, puzzled. "No more sport?" he asked.

Lydia shook her head. "It's not sport, it's. . . butchery." She had trouble breathing. She would never forget the apparition's touch.

At the next town, the conductor told the station agent that something mighty strange had happened during the run. The doctor was called, because two men and a lady had died of apparent heart failure or apoplexy. None of the passengers could or would say what happened, exactly. With no one to claim it, all the buffalo meat was sent to the local orphanage and the nearest Indian reservation.

###

About the Author

Salinda Tyson was born in Pennsylvania, lived a long time in Northern California, and now lives in Raleigh, North Carolina. Her story, "The Changing Table" appeared in *Shadows in Salem* this year, and Del Rey published her novel, *Wheel of Dreams,* in 1996.

*****~~~~~*****

La Loca

by Robert Walton

Sparks whirled like a dancer's skirts and then leaped toward December stars. The fire—manzanita below, oak on top—burned blue at its heart. Joaquin Murrieta extended his hands gratefully toward its fierce heat. His sixty-two years gave him appreciation for a good fire.

"Señor Murrieta, supper is ready."

Joaquin turned.

"Will you join me?" The speaker, a trim, bearded man in his middle years, gestured toward a long table beneath the portico of Dutton's Hotel. The table was laden with barbecued slabs of beef, roasted chickens, tortillas, preserves of apricots and plums, dishes of steamed squash and corn, jalapeños, cut lemons, pies, and cakes. A black iron pot of beans squatted at the table's far end.

Joaquin smiled, "I would be honored, Captain Dutton."

...

"Cigar?" Captain Dutton inclined his head.

Joaquin smiled. "Thank you, no."

"You enjoyed our modest feast?

"Very much so. I cannot resist roasted corn with butter and chilé."

Dutton waved expansively. "There is more!"

Now Joaquin laughed, "No! My horse must be able to carry me tomorrow!"

Dutton shrugged, plucked a cigar from his vest pocket, cut off its end with his penknife, and lit it with a match. Once its end was glowing, he said, "I would very much like you to extend your visit, sir. Jolón will be calmer once the fiesta ends." He gestured to the star-filled sky with his cigar. "And before the rains come, I promise you more California evenings such as this one."

A woman's scream, sharp as broken glass, suddenly rent the air. Figures struggled in darkness beyond the fire. The woman screamed again.

Joaquin and Dutton rose from their seats. Dutton lifted a lantern from the table's end, and they strode swiftly toward the disturbance. The lantern in Dutton's left hand made a swaying circle of yellow light on dry grass. He raised it and revealed a woman slumped on the ground. A compact, work-hardened man stood above her. Dutton asked, "What's the matter here?"

The man looked up. "This is none of your business, Captain."

Dutton's eyes glinted. "Michelson, isn't it?"

"What's it to you?"

Dutton continued in an even tone. "This is my property. Everything that happens here is my business."

"This woman gave me guff. I don't take guff from Mexicans. Or women." The man gripped a fistful of the woman's long, grey-streaked hair and pulled her face toward the light. The face was round, middle-aged and tear-stained. A bruise was already swelling beneath her left eye.

She sobbed, "Help me, Captain!"

"Shut up, bitch!" Michelson slapped her with his open right hand. Her head snapped to the side, and she whimpered.

Dutton shouted, "Unhand that woman!"

Michelson grabbed her hair, balled his hand into a fist, drew it back to punch her in earnest. Swifter than a stooping hawk, Joaquin stepped forward and gripped the fist with his left hand. Michelson's muscles bulged beneath his shirt as he strained against the old man's grip, but his hand didn't move. Anger replaced surprise on his face, and then fear froze his features into a snarl.

Joaquin nodded. "You had best do as Captain Dutton says."

Michelson released the woman's hair. Lantern light gleamed from Joaquin's neatly trimmed silver beard and from the silver blade he pressed into Michelson's armpit. A coin-sized patch of blood stained the man's shirt around the knife's tip.

Dutton smiled. "I want you off my property. Now."

Michelson glared at Dutton and then at Joaquin. Joaquin released Michelson's fist and stepped swiftly back, keeping his knife leveled before him. Michelson whirled and stalked into the darkness.

Dutton patted the crying woman's shoulder and offered her his other hand. "You are a Morales, no?"

"Yes, Señor Dutton." She took his hand and struggled to her feet.

"May we help you?"

Señora Morales smoothed her black skirt. "That man is after my niece, Rosinda." She looked down. "Perhaps Rosinda flirted with him, but she is only sixteen. She knows no better."

Dutton smiled grimly. "Do not fear, Señora Morales. Both you and your niece will be guarded tonight."

Joaquin asked, "Your niece is beautiful, Señora?"

Señora Morales looked at Joaquin. "As a flame, Señor."

...

Joaquin awoke suddenly. He felt for his boots with his left hand, found them. Sometimes, though with secret guilt, he slept with them on, even in a warm room, adobe walls awash in amber candlelight. Years of hunting and being hunted made his sleep a fragile cup, less than half full. Footsteps approached. They'd awakened him. A knock rattled his door.

"Mr. Murrieta?" Dutton's voice was hoarse.

"I'm here."

"There's trouble in the fiesta camp."

"I'm coming."

...

They walked beneath early winter stars, points of frozen blue fire, Dutton slightly ahead of Joaquin. A boy carrying a lantern walked ahead of him. Dutton spoke over his shoulder. "I posted two sentries tonight. Manuel here is only fourteen, but he's responsible. He woke me."

Manuel stopped abruptly and held the lantern low. Dutton and Joaquin stepped to either side of him. A dead man lay at their feet. His eyes were wide with surprise, and his mouth was open. Blood seeped into dust from a wound in the back of his head.

Joaquin asked, "Who is this man?"

"Clinton Burke, the other sentry." Dutton paused. "He served with me in the war."

"Michelson?"

Dutton nodded, "Michelson."

"The girl?"

Dutton nodded again. "He has her."

"We ride?" Joaquin asked.

Dutton straightened, looked at the sky. "It is several hours until dawn. We can gather men and follow him then."

Manuel dropped the lantern. It shattered on a rock and went out. "Señor!" he gasped, "Look!" The boy's shaking finger pointed into the darkness.

A tall woman approached from the river. Her face was pale and luminous. Her blue gown and shawl shone like moonlit ice. Her hair was midnight black. Dutton whispered, "La Loca."

Joaquin glanced at him. "La Loca?"

Manuel uttered a strangled cry and ran.

Dutton took a deep breath. "Do you fear ghosts, Mr. Murrieta?"

"I fear the evil which spawns them."

"Much evil created La Loca."

Joaquin remained silent.

Dutton continued, "She lived near Mission San Antonio when I first arrived in this territory. She was a beauty. All of the men in this valley, young and old, were drawn to her. She dallied with some of them. Her husband caught her with a young man. Though he had many lovers himself, he was jealous. When he accused her, she laughed at him. He squeezed her throat so hard that the prints of his fingers were branded into her flesh. Then he cut off her head."

Joaquin looked at Dutton. "Why?"

"He buried it in a hidden place so that her spirit could not rest."

"And?"

Dutton sighed. "Her spirit did not rest. She appeared first on the night after her Mass of burial. We found her husband's body the next day in front of his cabin."

Joaquin waited for Dutton to finish.

"His body was torn to pieces. The Indians say that monsters do her bidding." Dutton looked at Joaquin. "When La Loca appears, someone dies. Always."

La Loca stopped and looked directly at them. Her eyes were black pits in which embers gleamed. She raised her right hand and pointed toward the northwest.

Dutton's voice quavered, "We have a guide. Will you ride with me, sir?"

"Let us get our horses."

...

They rode up the old cattle trail toward Reliz Canyon, Joaquin slightly ahead of Dutton. La Loca drifted far ahead, but neither man sat easily in his saddle. An hour before dawn, the ghost vanished. Joaquin smelled wood smoke and held up his hand.

Dutton reined his horse in and leaned close to Joaquin. "What is it?"

"A campfire. You said Michelson has a gang. How many?"

"Six, perhaps seven."

Joaquin nodded. "We'll tie our horses here and approach them from below. The air is cold and flows downhill. Their horses will not smell us. The darkness will help us, too."

Dutton whispered, "Will there be a sentry?"

Joaquin pulled out his knife. "Always."

...

The sentry's fingers quivered, but he no longer breathed. Joaquin wiped his knife upon the man's wool jacket and sheathed it.

Dutton asked, "What now?"

"We find the girl and take her." Joaquin smiled. "If we can."

A rifle shot crashed from the left. Dutton cried out and fell to the ground. More shots sounded, and small flashes of gunpowder lightning lit the campground. A bullet sizzled past Joaquin's right ear. He fired his pistol at the flashes and dove to the ground near Dutton. The firing ceased.

Dutton gripped his leg and writhed in pain. Joaquin hissed, "Hold still!"

Dutton took a shuddering breath and froze.

Michelson shouted from above. "Garcia, around to the left! Thompson, hold where you are!"

Joaquin asked, "Are you badly hurt?"

Dutton snarled, "Yes, damn it!"

Joaquin grinned. "But not dying, I think. There was a second sentry."

"Obviously." Dutton wadded up a kerchief and bound it to his thigh with his belt.

"Can you shoot?"

Dutton grimaced. "I can shoot."

"Good. I'll move. When they fire at me, take them."

Dutton gripped his pistol. "Right."

Joaquin scrambled six steps to his left and dove into the shadow of a chamisa bush. Rifles crashed and bullets nipped at his heels. Dutton fired. One of Michelson's men cried out in agony.

Michelson rose and shouted, "Rush them now! Get them!" Strands of white light suddenly flared next to him, became La Loca. Her long fingers reached for him. He gasped and emptied his gun into her face, the heavy crashes rolling down the valley.

She smiled and caressed his cheek once. Then she seized him, held him fast and bent down until her lips nearly touched his.

Michelson screamed as he looked into her eyes. His scream tore his vocal chords to bloody rags, but he tried to scream again. La Loca released him. He fell to the ground, curled up, covered his eyes with both hands, and rolled from side to side, frothing and gurgling.

Rosinda moaned. She lay wrapped in blankets close to the fire. La Loca walked to her, bent down and caressed the girl's hair. She whispered into Rosinda's ear and then straightened. Snarls ripped the night. Great cats from a different age stepped from between boulders and approached the camp. Fangs longer than daggers distended their upper jaws, curved wickedly below their muzzles and shone with a silvery light of their own.

Joaquin murmured, "What are they?

"Tigers—they lived here long ago."

La Loca pointed toward Michelson's men. Eyes bulging, the gang members turned and ran. The tigers leapt after them. Howls of terror and pain sounded in the near darkness.

After a few moments, the tigers appeared again, heads swaying and fangs dripping. The ghost then turned toward Dutton and Joaquin. Joaquin held his breath.

She smiled at them, gestured again, and the tigers paced away. Still smiling, La Loca became a fountain of silver light and disappeared.

Joaquin rose and walked warily to Rosinda. He reached the girl and asked, "Are you all right?"

She nodded.

Joaquin knelt beside her. "La Loca spoke to you. What did she say?"

Rosinda whispered, "*Justicia.*"

Joaquin leaned forward. "Justice?"

"All women hope for justice." Rosinda looked up and smiled. "La Loca requires it."

Joaquin stared down the frosted vale. The saber-toothed tigers paced toward distant trees. Moonlight silvered rippling muscles. The last and greatest tiger looked back at Joaquin and then stepped beneath oak shadows.

###

About the Author

Robert Walton used real-life bandit Joaquin Murrieta as his protagonist in "La Loca," drawing inspiration for the story from Monterey County history and legend. This story placed in the 2012 *Saturday Writers* competition and subsequently appeared in the contest anthology.

The Gleaming

by John J. Kennedy

I half-dreamed a terrible screech, a banshee wail of derailed wheels, my eyes snapping open as the carriage lifted and plummeted, my mind clawing for something, anything. . . the tracks in this part of Nevada facilitated travel at almost thirty miles per hour; could we survive a crash at such ungodly speed? A terrible crunch as the floor lurched, cases and valises tumbling, one spilling a wad of dollar bills and jewellery. We rolled, and I sprawled out of my seat, something tugging at my jacket collar, half-choking me, arresting my flight. Glass sprayed and timbers creaked as we rumbled at last to a stop. My head snapped forwards and back again, that same something pulling me back into my seat with unfeasible strength.

I sat, gulping, and blinked around me. A large figure leaned back, left arm trailing, a limb bigger than any I'd seen on man, animal, or tree. Strangely attired; a faded Union tunic with an enlarged patchwork sleeve, a poncho, narrow-brimmed black beaver-fur hat, and completing the incongruity, a pair of brown fur lace-up boots, Native American style, over uncommonly large feet. Yet I had barely noticed him; hat pulled down and sleeping perhaps when I had entered the restaurant car earlier. Now, I was staring. "My deepest thanks to you sir. . . " I began.

"Ain't nothin'," he said, eyes darting up at the lopsided door. "Get y'head down!"

There were two of them, and if they were bandits then they were successful ones; gabardine coats, pearl-handled revolvers, neck-scarf masks crisp and well-laundered. They turned, pistols training on us, a shot careening past my cheek and heading straight for my newfound acquaintance—except he was no longer there. He seemed to have sprung across the length of the carriage, landing near our two assailants with a flex of his oversized feet, his arm swinging out from beneath the poncho and swatting one of them back through the door.

The other managed a shot, glancing off that same arm with a dull clang, the large gloved hand at the end of it closing on the pistol, barrel bending like a wilted flower, pearl-handle snapping into slivers.

The assailant backed away, but my acquaintance's arm flashed out, the black gloved hand fastening on his lapel and lifting him until his head met the lopsided ceiling of the carriage once, twice, a third time. As the arm moved, the patchwork fabric around it popped, and my jaw hung at the glint of burnished metal spokes and pulleys rather than skin. As he dropped his assailant, I fancied I could hear the whir of mechanics and the hiss of a piston released.

"They seen y'face, feller." Oddly marsupial bounding steps brought him to my side. "Best y'come wit'." With that, he pulled me to the window, knocking out loose shards with the large gloved hand. Then, in a move speedy as it was improbable, he clasped me around the waist and boosted us both through the empty frame. A few more springing strides and another jump took us over the trees, the rails snaking away to the haze of the horizon. I found a dry scream erupting from my innards as we plummeted towards the ground, my companion slanting us so that his feet alone absorbed the impact, producing a spray of steam which quickly dissipated beneath our legs as we hurtled skyward again.

I am proud to say I managed to keep my luncheon in place for almost another three bounds.

...

We stopped once to break our fifty-six miles "by jump," and I expected some account of my companion's outlandish abilities, but instead received some dried jerky, some water, and a name: Lloyd.

Later, as Lloyd excused himself behind some trees, I confess I peeped into his pack. A folded apparatus glistened there; I fancied I could see metallic fingers through its pulleys and gyres. A spare arm? But it looked far too small to fit him. I even confided in him about my impending marriage, a union long-arranged and awaited by my family and that of Daphne, my fiancé. I avoided mentioning my father's recent death and the financial straits we were in. As I extolled the virtues of a woman I had met once, as a three-year-old, he sat still save for the occasional ejection of black tobacco-spittle and then fixed me with a stare I couldn't fathom, telling me he'd deliver me at my destination, but via Reno, for he first had some "errands" to run.

And so, a few hours later my strange companion left me with a solemn "Adios!" near the telegraph office, and I wondered if he was abandoning me. But then he turned, repeating the details of our rendezvous tomorrow. I watched his strange bouncing gait as he disappeared into the steady flow of Reno townsfolk.

It was only because the *Wanted* poster flapped as I passed that my attention fell on it. The hat was accurately drawn, the sun-browned face less so, but it was undoubtedly my companion. Lloyd Henry Malcolm, wanted for robbery of a gold shipment near Tuscon and a stagecoach hold-up in Wyoming. No mention of his unusual abilities other than in the single word:

Dangerous! I shook my head. I had fallen into the company of an outlaw.

Something not quite right in that surmise, though. I thought of the carriage and the opened valise scattering dollar bills and jewels into the air as we had tumbled to a halt. Yet Lloyd's focus had remained resolutely on getting me a safe distance from danger; hardly the actions of a lawbreaker.

I chewed my lip, turning from the poster to the sight of two expensive gabardine coats and familiar neck-scarves outside the window. I fanned my face with my hat and busied myself with a newspaper, glancing up again to see their shrinking backs crossing the street and following in Lloyd's wake.

I stepped out and watched them trail him into the saloon.

I idled, uncertain what to do. The two gabardine-wearing hunters would recognize me if I entered the bar, and if I was to stand here breathing the dusty air of Reno's main thoroughfare much longer, the same would likely be true.

I turned. There was a hotel directly opposite, *The Marigold*, and I stared at its battered signage for a second, straightened up, and strode in, taking a room upstairs.

One of my hobbies is bird watching, a pastime I shan't detail here, other than it has afforded me a rather impressive collapsible telescope which I keep upon my person. Taking it now, I positioned a chair near the window and peered across the street through the windows of the saloon. I found him, sitting upstairs. I half-expected some scene of physical debauchery, but that was, as it turned out, not Lloyd's vice. Instead, cigar smoke swirling, a decanter of whisky close to his right hand, Lloyd was focused on the hand of cards fanned in front of him.

...

I awoke half sprawled against the chair to noises from across the road. Cursing myself for abandoning my vigil, I went downstairs and out into the darkened street, crossing quickly and turning into the alley to the side of the saloon.

A cart stood there, unusually fashioned. Upon its back, surely made to purpose, was a large iron bathtub. The cart's two horses eyed me as I passed, but made no noise. I hoisted myself up onto the back of the cart and peered down into the bath.

Lloyd was in his long johns, their legs ripped at the bottoms to accommodate his large metallic feet and calves, glistening bronze in the reflected sodium lamp that cornered the alley. His torso was bare, and his oversized left arm was fully exposed, farther magnified by the water he lay in, fully mechanical from shoulder to fingertips, an intricate lattice of pistons, gyres, and pulleys, but inactive. Lloyd's other, *human* hand was tied to this one, anchored. He was immobile other than the eyes flickering up at me, a long groan escaping his miserable lips.

For a moment I felt no pity. Whisky fumes were apparent, surely explaining his capture. But then such was the exasperation and shame in his countenance that I relented. I reached down to try the fastening but he shook his head. "The plug!"

I crouched, plunging my hand in between his mechanical ankles and finding the bung, wasting my strength pulling for a few seconds, then turning it anti-clockwise. It was stiff. Sudden voices rang from the main street and Lloyd's whisper was a hiss. "Quick! They catch ya here, like as not they'll kill ya."

Intended as incentive or not, it worked; the plug creaked free with my redoubled effort. I shuffled into the darkness beneath the bath and hid, the water sluicing through the pipes above me.

I heard the two gunmen climbing up onto the seat, a flap of the reins, "Giddyap!" I gave silent thanks they hadn't chosen to gloat over their captive, but no sooner had the thought passed than the creaking boards of the cart revealed one had chosen to do exactly that, even with the journey under way. His bootheels were planted wide, surprise evident in his indrawn breath and muttered "Sonofa. . . !" His pistol dragged against the leather of his holster, and there was a groan of frustration from Lloyd, his limbs clearly still inoperative.

My feet kicked out almost of their own accord, catching the gunman's shins and sending him sprawling off the cart down onto the passing track. Even as I heard his muffled cries, I shook my head at what I had just done. If these were truly lawmen, I had just made myself an accessory to a fugitive's escape.

A gunshot rang out, high. Another. Then another. The cart slowed, presumably as the driver realized his compadre's predicament. Now what to do?

A sudden clang as an oversized metallic foot scraped the bath and clawed a hold on the wood of the cart, then a cacophony of wrenching, rivets popping, wood creaking.

"Stay down!" Lloyd said, upending the bath, swinging it round just as more gunshots came from the front. The horses whinnied, and we were moving again. I had a glimpse of Lloyd rushing the driver, the bath deflecting his shots in white sparks, Lloyd's arm swiping him off the cart, then Lloyd re-angling his makeshift shield to cover his back as he took the reins. His cries of "Whoa there!" echoed dully in the iron bath as we careered through the town and out onto pure prairie.

. . .

"Yup. They want my invention bad," Lloyd said, as we approached what looked like a plantation and mining settlement, two hours later. "Almost had me once 'fore, when I fell into a creek back at Cheyenne. Cold water stops the pistons. Guess they remembered."

I nodded, regarding the collapsed mine entrance, clearly blasted by a much earlier explosion. "So, this is it?"

Lloyd had finally divulged something of his past on our little trip across the prairie. He'd been an engineer, well respected, for the Union Pacific Railroad and later for many of the mines in the area, until the accident that had taken his arm and legs.

I frowned. "One thing I don't understand. You're clearly an exceptional engineer," I indicated his arm and legs, "and an inventor the like of which this world has never seen. But how on earth were you able to see your. . . creation. . . to fruition with only one working hand?"

He grinned at me, I think perhaps for the first time. "I'd already made me some prototypes. Was plannin' to use 'em fer mine-work, controlled from a distance by what I was gonna call *telegraph without wires*." He shrugged. "Anyways, weren't too difficult to redesign 'em to fit me. But as fer the fine tunin'. . . " He looked soulful now, stopping the cart and nodding at the shack set back from the other buildings. "Had me some help."

She came from the doorway as if called for, the basket of laundry under her arm.

She was fine, in a way I was entirely unaccustomed to. Her native skin was brown, and the braided length of her black, black hair trailed down over her shoulder. No smile, no coquetry or polite civility. A glance at me and then a long appraising look at Lloyd, and though she did not move I could tell she was laboring; fire in her heart but not quite ready to send signals with it.

Lloyd was stoic, only a churning at his temples revealing the emotion he must have felt. "Ayasshe," he said simply.

She stared a moment, glanced at me again, then, just as Lloyd coughed and was probably about to introduce me, she shook her head. "You shouldn't have come." She eyed the big house at the center of the plantation and turned her other side to us, the empty sleeve of her buckskin dress flapping as she walked away.

Her right arm, I realized with a jolt, finished just below the shoulder.

I stared at Lloyd. "*She* was your helper. Injured in the explosion too?"

He stared at the ruined mineshaft. "Shouldna been there. Wuz bringin' me some lemonade. Back then she wuz just a maidservant here. Now. . . " He looked at his oversized feet. "God knows what they have her doin'."

I glanced at his pack. "But why haven't you given her a new arm? Taken her out of here?"

"Cause I ran out o' gold 'fore it was finished!" He gritted his teeth and spat, tears in his eyes. "Cause I'm a fool. An' a bad gambler. An' a drunk."

I looked down.

"But. . . Ayasshe. Why—why did she look up at the house that way?"

He laughed coldly. "Time to blow the dust out y'eyes, Englishman. Think slavery ended fer everybody with that declaration twenny-five years back?" He nodded at the large house. "There's some fine people runnin' this place. One way or 'nother they make it hard fer some folk t'leave." He shook his head. "But you'll find out soon enough!"

I looked around me, slowly beginning to catch his meaning. "You mean this is Cedar Bluff? This is *my* destination too?"

Lloyd spat on the ground, walking away.

...

Our families had been close before Daphne's had chosen to invest in the colonies. They'd stayed in touch, never forgetting the union they'd agreed on. The house, the mine, the surrounding plantation would be worth a fortune, and it was mine to step into.

She met me in the lobby of the big house, glancing at my disheveled appearance and casting her eyes down. It cut through any doubt I may still have had. Her duty may have had the potential to one day translate her indifference to passion, or something counterfeiting it, but Daphne's eyes were her truth. They would never hold for me what Ayasshe's had held for Lloyd a few moments ago. Never in this world.

...

It was as I walked dejectedly back towards the workers' shack that the gunshots cracked. I started running, the rocks at the edge of the old mineshaft giving me cover. From here, I could already see a crowd gathering around the two figures in gabardine jackets, their bodies broken, a large boulder having rolled to a stop behind them. But where was Lloyd?

I heard shuffling from inside the shaft. I crept in.

He was on his knees, cradling the arm from his pack. Blood welled beneath him from two large wounds on his torso. He saw me, let out a dark laugh. "Guess they thought they'd settle for the invention *without* the inventor."

"Who sent them, Lloyd? Who was after your secret?"

He spat some blood. "One rich man or another. Don't matter."

I reached into my inside pocket, pulled out the ring I had brought from Golder's Green in London. I held it up. "This is for you, Lloyd. Maybe enough to buy materials, finish the arm for—"

He shook his head, pointing at his own mechanical arm, holding it up to shafts of daylight. For the first time I could see the gossamer lines that criss-crossed the pistons and gyres, glinting yellow. "The gold ain't fer the materials. The gold *is* the material."

Non-corrosive, malleable, and ductile. I was and am no scientist, but it made sense. I looked at my once-intended wedding ring. "Then it's enough?"

His smile became a wince, and he nodded. He handed me the arm. "Ayasshe knows the process."

The blood was coursing now, and he grinned despite it, moving his human hand to his pocket, bringing a book of matches from there. I saw the array of dynamite around him and stood.

"I was never worthy o' my talents." He stared up at the rock ceiling. "Worse, I let her down, bad." A glint as he glanced at me. "Take care o' her, Englishman!"

Golden light from the cracks caught his limbs, making a statue of him.

...

The process took three days. I hid out in the hills, came back down to the fence and waited. At ten, the sun behind her, she rode out on a strong looking horse, blanket, no saddle. Would they chase her for a horse-thief? Probably.

She nodded at me. It wasn't the look she'd given Lloyd. Not close. But it was something.

She pulled away, galloped off, her braid slapping her back as she rode.

I looked at the ground, then up at the rubble of the mineshaft and the grave it held, the secrets buried within it.

Hooves, closing. Then a grip strong as iron swept me up, off my feet, around behind her and I held onto her waist, her black braid whipping against my smile.

###

About the Author

John J. Kennedy teaches English at a college in the North East of England, though he's done plenty to earn a crust over the years, including peeling bulbs in Holland and busking round Europe. He has an MA in Creative Writing, and he's been shortlisted for *Albedo One's* Aeon prize and (for his other genre—Crime) for the CWA *Debut Dagger* for a first novel which he's currently knocking into shape, along with a sci-fi epic he's been tinkering with for years. His inspiration comes from the people he's met and the crazy things he's seen them do. He truly believes that if we remember that all human beings are fundamentally insane then nothing should surprise us too much, though he's constantly amazed by the support he gets from his wife and daughter.

*****~~~~~*****

Closing the Frontier

by Philip DiBoise

"She sure is a sight, ain't she," said the Mayor. "Makes me proud to be alive."

"Sure is a sight," said Dewey.

There were cowboys and Sioux. There were gunfighters and rustlers. There were gamblers in their fine French shirts, and there were blushing saloon girls with hearts of gold. They were all there, standing together, a great line out to the edge of town. All of them Dewey had ever read stories about, and they stood, bored, waiting for the bureaucrat's pen. It was a sight Dewey had never imagined man would see. He'd known they were closing the frontier, of course, but the black and white of copy was not the same as seeing. He only wished Junior could have gotten a gawk, but he and Mona weren't due for days. And by that time it would all be over, and the stories and the West would just be another place.

"Makes me glad you can see that," said the Mayor. "There'd be a lot of people from your parts who might lose. . . Well, perspective, as my pa would say."

The line was moving steadily forward, as it had been all day. But when the latest posse made it to the front and turned in their guns and torches and vengeful spirit, the sight, well, it was the same as the first time Dewey had seen them that morning. Not even hours spent under the sun and smelling the Mayor could take something like that away. And when the federal man checked his boxes, and had them sign on the line, it was as if something in the light grew dimmer. Well maybe not dimmer, but more familiar.

"Sure am glad y'all could do this today," said the Mayor. "You know we're having us an election next week. And well, you know. People'll be real happy to feel protected. And they'll remember I did it, when they're at the polls."

"Makes you proud to be alive," said Dewey.

"That it does," said the Mayor with a chuckle.

The last of the posse handed over their names, and were given factory time cards and shiny new Faris brand lunch pails. The new workers moved on, and a duelist with a mustache bordering on the excessive stepped forward. He was more than eager for a new life.

"If you ain't bothered," said the Mayor conspiratorially. "I do have a question."

"I've got all day," said Dewey.

"Well," said the Mayor looking around to make sure none of his constituents were close. "Well, you see. And of course men such as us. Well, we understand, but some of the others were asking. What I'm getting at here is. . . Well, does it really eat 'em after it kills 'em?"

"What?" asked Dewey.

"Well, now, of course I do understand how it works," said the Mayor quickly. "What with the boilers and the dials, and. . . and the gears and everything. And I was in the war too, of course. Did my duty. Seen them marching through the fields and such, but you see. . . The thing is, my service was much more what you might call. . . supportive than combative. And, well, I guess, I just ain't never actually seen one of them fight. And some of the older folks have been asking questions."

"Oh," said Dewey realizing he and the Mayor had been pondering two very different things.

"And it's glorious of course," continued the Mayor. "Makes me proud and all that like I said, but it's just hard to imagine something like that could be safe. And there is the matter of the election and whatnot."

Dewey looked over at the Manifestor, in whose shadow he and the Mayor were resting, and he was surprised to realize the Mayor was right. Long familiarity had dulled the monstrosity's effect. Dewey hadn't even remembered it was there.

It was a Mark 3 General Forge and Foundry Progresso line Manifestor. It was forty feet tall, and mostly wood. But the rest was brutality in brass and iron. Two long arms hung like an ape's, but they were tipped with rending claws which could toss a locomotive. Cannons stuck out from its shoulders, and a great smokestack rose from its spine. It had a face of sorts, a skull with glowing green eyes and square, horrendous teeth. Dewey could see why someone might think it ate the dead, but of course that was as foolish as men on the moon. It would never stop to eat.

"It's not safe," said Dewey. "That's the whole point."

The Mayor pulled an already soiled kerchief from his pocket and dabbed at the beads of sweat spattered across his great red forehead. Dewey would have rather watched the line, but civility won in the end.

"No," Dewey said. "It doesn't eat the dead. It only makes them."

"But," said the Mayor. "It is safe for us, right. I mean, you know, it's not gonna come for us in our homes."

Dewey knew what the Mayor was really asking, and as much as he wanted to watch the man squirm, he couldn't. Dewey remembered his first time standing beneath one of the great engines, and if he couldn't actually feel sympathy for the Mayor, a life in public relations had at least given him the ability to fake it. It was the one part of the job he was truly great at.

"No," said Dewey. "You'll be fine. It won't care about that sort of thing. It punishes those who break the law, but not small things. Feel free to spit in the street, if that's the way you feel, but I'd be sorry for the man who fires a gun in town. Old Progresso had a real issue with murderers, and he hardwired that straight into his children. Sort of ironic, if you ask me."

The Mayor didn't seem placated, but Dewey didn't have what the man wanted. Truly no man knew where the Manifestor would draw the line, but a better education would have served the Mayor. There was a Manifestor on every street in Washington. If they had a problem with crooked dealing, the capital would have returned to the swamp years ago. A man like the Mayor had nothing to fear.

"Your election will be fine," said Dewey.

"But—" began the Mayor, but Dewey raised a hand to stop him.

"It's all in the brochure," said Dewey.

"Yes, well," said the Mayor. "Of course, I've read your brochure, but some of our good people aren't much for letters, if you know what I mean."

"Well, that's why they have you," said Dewey.

The Mayor tried to chuckle again, but it was as hollow as his promises. Dewey handed the Mayor a brochure, and the fat man buried his nose in it.

Dewey was proud of the brochure. It said almost nothing, but within it was everything the Mayor needed to know. After all, it wasn't as if the man had a choice in the Manifestor. Decisions like that had been made far above the level of the Mayor.

It had been strategic in its way. GFF got its pieces of silver, the world got to be safe, and men like Dewey got to justify their educations. And if that meant every place got just a little more like Dewey's home, all the better for it. Rhode Island wasn't so bad. Dewey's eyes were drawn back to the line. It was almost over, and the Manifestor was idle. It was everything a company man was meant to want.

The line moved again as a group of prospectors turned speculators went on to make the world a more productive place, and that was when Dewey saw him. He was second to last, standing in front of a group of bandits who in a different time he would have hunted or maybe helped. The man was old and beaten down, but in his stride, and the worn yet still supple leather of his gunbelt, Dewey saw a whole life of adventure. The Mayor was still reading, and Dewey almost ran to the Gunslinger. Dewey's younger self would not let him miss something like that. It was everything he'd wanted to be.

The Gunslinger, and a man like that could have been nothing else, wore the miles of his life plainly. He was ragged at the edges, and his suit had been turned grey by time. Nothing like it ever would have been let into the offices back home. Old Mr. Myers would have sent a man in that suit home to change, and added a stern yet impotent mark on his file as the girls tittered about the man's wife. It was everything Dewey and his smart suits had always feared, but Dewey would have bet he was the only man in a hundred miles who cared. A life of not sitting in an office and worrying about Mona's parents and the rungs on a fanciful ladder had something to offer, even if Dewey couldn't tell what color the man's suit had originally been.

Dewey had been eager to speak with the Gunslinger, but now he had nothing to say. So in the end he stood next to the old man as if somehow he belonged, and he tried not to stare. The Gunslinger spat something yellow and glistening and turned towards Dewey with a cough.

"Yes," said the Gunslinger.

"Um, hello," said Dewey.

The Gunslinger pushed his hat from his eyes and looked Dewey over for a full three seconds before he spat again. This time it was green.

"Yes," repeated the Gunslinger.

"I was just wondering. . . " said Dewey but he trailed off.

"Yes," said the Gunslinger. "It's a mighty shame."

"You mean the closing of the frontier?" asked Dewey.

"No," said the Gunslinger. "I reckon that's a good, for what that's worth. I meant that beast over there."

"The Manifestor?" asked Dewey, thinking for a moment the Gunslinger meant the Mayor.

The Gunslinger let out a chuckle, which slowly rolled into a full laugh, but then collapsed into another bout of coughing. The Mayor was picking his nose, but Dewey didn't think that was near funny enough to make an archetype laugh.

"What's so funny?" Dewey asked.

"Men," said the Gunslinger after he'd wiped his mouth on a crusty sleeve.

"How so?" asked Dewey.

"Only men would come up with a name for something that don't need one."

"So, what would you call it?" asked Dewey.

"What it is," said the Gunslinger.

Dewey stared at the man, but the Gunslinger didn't seem one for needless jawing. The line moved forward, and the end grew closer. Dewey knew something important was slipping through his fingers, but he didn't have words for what it was.

"Why's it a good?" asked Dewey. "I mean, don't you want to stay?"

"'Course I do," said the Gunslinger. "But that don't matter none."

Dewey waited and finally, after the line had moved yet another space forward, the Gunslinger sighed.

"It's savage and wild, and it changes you," the Gunslinger said. "It's everything it needed to be, but we don't need that no more. It's just you and your monsters and jobs now."

"But," began Dewey, but there was too much, and not enough to say. The Mayor had finished his business and was headed over to join them. The line moved forward again, and Dewey and the Gunslinger had only one person between them and the federal man's table.

"Time's almost up," said the Gunslinger.

"I just," began Dewey as the Mayor got close. "I just don't understand why you all lined up. You couldn't have won, but not one of you tried to fight. I don't get it."

With one finger the Gunslinger pushed the brim of his hat up as he thought, and the Mayor actually leaned forward to listen.

"Ain't no point," the Gunslinger said. "It's been coming a long time. I've been out here fifty years. Gave my youth, and my sons. It's yours now. I ain't gonna fight for that."

The line moved, and Dewey stepped out as the Gunslinger approached the small table. He didn't say anything but unfastened his gun belt and slammed it down. The federal man looked through his papers and passed them forward for the Gunslinger to sign.

"I must say," said the Mayor. "I really did think we'd be seeing something. Made a bet and everything."

"I guess," said Dewey. "I guess they're all just ready."

The Gunslinger leaned down to read his contract with tired eyes, and behind him the bandits started to yell. They'd been growing agitated as they moved towards the front, and it seemed they'd finally had enough.

"I ain't doing this," one of them yelled as he pulled his gun. "This ain't how I go."

The bandit fired his gun, and one of the fresh workers fell in a heap. It took a second, but the rest of the bandits stepped out of line and went about their trade. There was screaming and hollering, and the bandits fired indiscriminately and accurately. Dewey knew he should have been scared, but the Gunslinger standing next to him, his hand still poised and about to sign, was smiling.

"What in the name of creation is this?" bellowed the Mayor, but he dove behind the table when one of the bandits looked his way.

Bullets were firing all around, and blood and bodies littered the street, but the Gunslinger reached into his pocket and began to meticulously roll himself a cigarette. The Manifestor groaned as the great snake oil boilers in its stomach started to burn. It belched a great cloud of green black smoke from its stack, but, as is the nature of all such great and powerful things, it took longer than it needed to react.

"I guess some people don't change," said Dewey almost to himself.

"I could give a bull's dangling sack about people," shouted the Mayor. "Don't just stand there. They're killing my voters."

"What would you have me do?" asked Dewey.

"Get that beast of yours killin," shouted the Mayor. "Do something. Anything."

The Gunslinger took a step to the side just as a man running behind him was shot dead, and he scowled as he worked at the tobacco.

"It takes time for the boilers to heat up," said Dewey. "It's all in the brochure."

"To damnation with your brochure," spat the Mayor, sticking his head out just long enough to see another voter gunned down. "You made the beast, didn't you?"

"I'm not an engineer," said Dewey. "I made the brochure."

"So what good are you?" hollered the Mayor.

"None," said Dewey, and the Gunslinger grunted a chuckle.

With his cigarette finally rolled, the Gunslinger slowly lit it, and made his decision. The federal man was shaking in his chair, holding his ledger with its big seal protectively in front of him like a talisman. The Gunslinger reached out two worn red gloves and pulled his guns from their holsters. Dewey raised a hand as if he could change what was going to happen, but the Gunslinger turned, a grin on his face twelve miles wide.

Bam.

The first bandit was dead.

Bang, Pop, Crack. Three more hit the ground.

The Gunslinger seemed to stand full for the first time, and as he stretched his shoulders a symphony of snaps and cracks rolled like thunder. The Mayor stuck his head out from his hiding place, and this time he kept watching. The show was good enough for even a man like him to risk something.

There were five more shots quick as an industrial hammer, and five more bandits were without their lives.

It was the most impressive thing Dewey had ever seen. The guns were like a brush or a pen in the Gunslinger's hands. There was no doubt or wavering. He erased his quarry with all the hesitation and mercy of a copy editor who spotted a split infinitive. Some men were put on the earth for one purpose, and Dewey had not realized what that actually meant until he saw.

Behind him, the Mayor was dabbing at his sweaty brow with his already dripping handkerchief, and so he missed it when the Manifestor first began to move.

The men on the lines back in Rhode Island were good at their jobs. Untold tons of brass and iron and Brazilian hardwood strode forward. Every step burned enough fuel to feed a family of nine, but the behemoth couldn't care about something like that.

Dewey knew the tremor when he felt it, but the Gunslinger wouldn't have listened even if Dewey had cared to yell. The guns fired three more times, and the last of the bandits were done. The Gunslinger spun his empty guns around his fingers and tried to put them into their holsters with a well-rehearsed move. Of course, his holster was back on the table, and so, when the Gunslinger turned, he had a sheepish half smile on his face. He looked like he had something to say, but he never got the chance.

Dewey had just enough time to see the joy in the old Gunslinger's eyes, before, with a tremendous crash like the slamming shut of some colossal book, the Manifestor's foot came down, and the last Gunslinger was no more.

"Well tan my hide and call me bacon," the Mayor said. "Greatest thing I ever saw."

The Manifestor groaned and walked slowly back to wait next to the train station. Dewey tried not to look at where the Gunslinger had been, but he couldn't help himself.

"Could we," began the Mayor excitedly. "I mean, could we put bunting and such on it? You know, for the election."

"Bunting costs extra," said Dewey.

###

About the Author

Third Flatiron welcomes another talented newcomer, Philip DiBoise. A senior at Santa Clara University, he has been writing actively for three years, and recently began to submit his work for publication.

*****~~~~~*****

No County For Young Men

by Martin Clark

It rained. It surely did.

Not that I minded, as where I was raised you chewed dust nine months of the year. I sat on the boardwalk outside Fain's Dry Goods, under the first-floor overhang. The streets of Gibson's Reach were rivers of mud, pure and simple. People glanced at me then looked away, but I was used to that. I got this big strawberry birthmark as covers half my face, and it unsettles some. Been that way my whole life. One of them new steam-carriages slithered by, towed by a team of six mules. Made me smile.

I used an upturned apple barrel as a table, cleaning the induction coil on my old Volta. Called her 'Rosie.' Truth is she named herself; I wasn't one to disagree. Some folks tell you guns ain't got real smarts, it's just tricksy responses. Well, my Rosie's got a mean streak, rattlesnake mean, the mean you only get from a lifetime of bitterness and regret. You ain't gonna' tell me some fancy-pants coder back East put *that* in a gun, no sirree.

Barney Huckster leaned against the railing, watching. I didn't like Barney Huckster, but he was too dumb to notice. He had a heavy gut and weak eyes that watered behind thick spectacles. Barney Huckster was a jerk.

The sound of spurs on the boards made us look round. It was a tall man in duster and hat, water pooling around his boots as he stood, looking at me. "You'll be the one they call Red Mahler?"

Even though Rosie was in pieces, I made a show of standing, empty hands, before replying. "Yes, sir, that would be me."

He nodded. "I'm Bert Miller. Josh is my youngest. I heard tell of some foolishness between you and him over one of Miss Markham's girls back in Mishap."

"Yes, sir. He beat up on her, so I beat up on him."

Old man Miller removed his hat and shook it. He had grey hair worn to the shoulder and eyes the color of cornflowers. "I told them, told all four of them, that it ain't worth a hanging, not over a whore. So it's just Josh as come after you, boy, and you ain't run near far enough. He still can't ride but wouldn't wait once word came in you was holed up here. I thought it would be done by now, and I was aiming to smooth things over with the Law. Given you'd be dead and he might be in jail."

Barney smiled, real nervous. "It's the weather, sir. Stage can't manage the incline this side of the ferry. Didn't you pass it?"

The tall man shook his head. "Had me some business in Pendleton, so that took me round by way of the long bridge." He frowned at me. "I'd tell you to clear out, boy, but I never seen Josh this riled before, and he'd got his Ma's temper. I'm not here to stand between the two of you, I'm here to take him home afterwards—we clear on that?"

I nodded. "Yes, sir. Appreciate it."

"Fine, now, I'll be having a drink while we wait. Send your boy here to fetch me soon as Josh shows up. I'll try and keep things civilized." Miller turned and walked down the street, heading for the Fair Hand Saloon.

Barney spat on the boardwalk, but quiet like, so as not to draw attention. "I ain't your boy, no how." He hitched up his breaches. "You really gonna' fight Josh Miller over some whore?"

I sat down, knot in my gut like bad vittles. "Come across Lucile getting whaled on, man using his fists. She liked me, least ways she looked me in the eye when we spoke. So grabbed a length of timber and busted it over his shoulders, 'fore I realised who it was. Stomped his leg so he couldn't ride and got the hell out of Mishap that very night."

"I get that, the Millers own that town, Sheriff and all. But why you stop runnin'? Ain't more than two days ride."

"Gets rowdy around here come the weekend, ranch hands blowing off steam, so you got a Sheriff and a Deputy. Them there Miller boys stick together like rats in a drain. Four of them agin me, that's murder, pure and simple. I figured the Law wouldn't stand for it, send them on their way. Walter Gibson runs things here, and ain't no love lost 'tween him and Bert Miller. I figured I was safe."

Barney grunted. "Well, you figured wrong."

I nodded and lifted Rosie. "I figured wrong." The Volta had cost me twenty dollars cash money back in Grumman. Seemed like a lifetime ago. So far Rosie and me had killed three men, a Mexican, and a steer that crept up on me sudden. Not that Barney knew squat about me before I showed up in Gibson's Reach. I slid the coil back together and locked the housing in place.

I carried Rosie over to the open window and connected her to the power feed Mister Fain let me use for sweeping the store. Her regulator was a poor repair, meaning I only got five, maybe six, shots from a charge. Now, each one would burn a hole in you the size of my fist, but an Edison or Tesla were good for twenty spikes or more.

It took a few moments for her to spin up. "So, boy, where we at?" She had a nasal Texas whine that riled most folks.

"Still in Gibson's Reach, Rosie. Roads are so bad I couldn't even clear Ghent County if I wanted, let alone reach the state line."

"She-*it*, so, what, you fixin' to become a permanent resident of Boot Hill?"

"Well, it was either face my trouble here or have it catch me on the hop down the trail some. I had a plan."

"Dammit, boy, what did I say about leaving the thinking to me." She sighed, "Take it things didn't pan out?"

"Nope."

"Figures. How many gunning for you *this* time?"

"Just the one—Josh Miller."

"Long streak of nothin'? Bad temper?"

"That's him."

"And they say a man can't chose his enemies. Now, let me rest and figure things out. I'm gonna' need every ounce of juice."

I let her be and sat down. Barney stood and worried on a hang nail like it was prime rib. Time passed. Always does. He scratched himself.

"Why you stick with a hunk o' metal like that, Red? Takes both hands just to lift the damn thing."

I looked up at him and his gap-toothed smile. "I figure if you shoot someone, do them the courtesy of treating it serious. I wouldn't disrespect a man by ending his life with a goddam derringer, like some."

Barney's face went sour. His Ma beat him black-and-blue for wasting money on a gravel-voiced Edison—a weapon no self-respecting gunslinger would ignore. So now he carried a pissant Ohm two-shot with a little-girl lisp. Heard tell Barney gut-shot a man in a dispute over cards up in No-Name City, and it took him three days to die. He sniffed. "Dead is dead, don't matter how. You think Josh Miller won't use that Gauss rifle of his if he gets the chance? He'll bushwhack you, for sure."

"Not in this. They say he can drive nails at a hundred yards, but out *there*. . . " I gestured with my chin ". . . you can't see more than twenty feet."

Barney looked out at the curtain of falling water. Even the buildings right across the street were hazy and indistinct. "Can't rain forever. Unless you're kin to Noah."

We waited. The stage couldn't get any closer than the Kirkwall spread, a good four miles away. The passengers had taken shelter there, and Al Kirkwall had slithered his way in to let us know everyone was safe. The boy didn't have the sense he was born with. So Mister Fain said, and it was hard to disagree. If a ropey kid like Al Kirkwall could make it up the long slope from the ferry, then maybe Josh could as well, bad leg or none.

Just sitting, it sure got under my skin. Cleared my throat. "I seen the innards of a pistol once, back-a-ways when I worked in Bauxite, Harrison County. Hank Lehman dropped his Faraday in the street, and it got crushed under a mining wagon. I seen little cards no bigger than a fingernail, cogs and wheels like from a pocket watch, red oil soaking into the dirt. Looked like blood. Bunch of us took it to old Mister Landa, who ran the pawn shop and fixed clocks. Shook his head and said he couldn't do nothing for her, got all teared up. Paid Hank ten dollars and didn't even use it for parts. Buried it out back, like it was a dog or something. When he carried it away, I swear all the guns in the display case, they all sighed, no word of a lie. Made the hair on my neck stand up, for sure." I trailed off, mouth dry. Not used to talking that much.

Barney stared at me, brows down low. "Say what?"

Felt my face color up. "Just saying, is all. Guns—"

Raised voices across the street made us both look. Josh Miller stood there; no hat, hair plastered to his skull, using his long rifle as a crutch. He'd been rolling in the mud some. Josh was arguing with Violet Parma, from the

Circle-K. She wore breaches and boots like her brothers and had more balls than both of them put together. Her and Josh were walking out back when I stayed in Mishap, although folks said it was more what the families wanted than them being sweethearts. Handsome girl, in her way, but nobody I'd want to cross.

Josh, though, he wouldn't know a good thing if it bit him in the ass. He got fresh before the nuptials, and then some. The Miller boys were used to getting what they wanted, but Violet, hell, she kneed Josh in the nethers and left him lying in his own sick. Neither family wanted a range war and tried to act like the betrothal never happened. Well, it sure looked like they still had business to settle.

I stood up, wiped my hands on my jeans. "Best go fetch Mister Miller, Barney. Quick now."

He scurried away while I watched Violet and her old beau argue back and forth. Less than a minute and I heard spurs on the boards. Bert Miller stepped up beside me, Barney at his shoulder.

Violet jabbed Josh in the chest with her finger, making some point. He slapped her, hard, sent her back a step. But she didn't cry out, or even raise a hand to her cheek. Just spat blood on the boardwalk, turned, and strode into Baskins Hardware. I heard the Gauss rifle giggle; a high-pitched sneer with a crazy-person edge to it. Some guns, hell, it's like they enjoy the hurt.

Bert Miller sighed. "Damn that boy, he'll be the death of me yet." The tall man looked me up-and-down, shook his head. "Best ready that antique of yours, son. I'll let Josh know to wait until you're able to step out." He set off across the street—the long way, using the boards some civic-minded soul had laid across the mud.

Barney wiped his mouth. "You want me to go fetch the Sheriff? Try to, at least?"

I shook my head. "Nah, one place is as good as another when you're in the ground." I lifted Rosie from the windowsill and held her close to my ear, listening to the soft *schlick* and *whirr* that always sends a shiver down my spine. My hand didn't shake none as I freed her from the cable. Proud of that. I felt the dull-point needles extend from the handle of my gun. Rosie used them to apply pressure, to guide my hand.

"Now you listen, boy, and listen good." She sounded almost gentle, "You ain't never drew-down before, deliberate like, it's always been in the moment. Well, don't matter shit who fires first, it only matters who's left standing. No shame in killing a man fair and square, don't let anyone tell you different. You hear?"

"I hear."

"Uh-huh, well, get ready. Rude to keep a man waiting for his own funeral."

Across the way I could see Josh and his Pa talking. Josh handed over the rifle and took his father's long-barreled Tesla in exchange. The Gauss was caked in mud, and I figure he didn't want it blowing up in his face. Despite the rain Josh fished out a pair of black glass spectacles from inside his coat and hooked them in place. They had sides, like the blind wear to hide empty eyes. Once I heard a man in Bauxite talking about 'thermals'—said they let a gun see heat, improved its aim.

Josh gestured with the Tesla towards the empty street. I checked the pocket watch in my waistcoat, but it had stopped. Barney passed me my hat. I left my coat over the back of the chair, walked along until I was standing in front of the Celestial Bathhouse.

We stepped down from the opposite boardwalks. The mud came half way up my boots, holding me fast like I was glued in place. The few townsfolk about stopped to watch rather than take cover. Gibson's Reach wasn't the place where you saw much in the way of gunplay.

It was Friday. I figured Mister Chang would be getting ready for those ranch hands who wanted a bath. I figured that if Josh *could* see heat then standing in front of the bathhouse boiler, just through the wall behind me, would even things out.

We faced each other, guns hanging by our sides. The Volta felt like an anvil. The rain beat on my hat so hard it sounded like small stones. My shoulders were damp. All I could see was Josh Miller. He smiled, I didn't.

I dragged that big old pistol up to shoulder height, ignored the pain in my wrist, clamped my other hand around the butt as well. Josh twisted sideways, making himself a smaller target, gun up and steady.

Rosie pushed at my palm, urging my aim away from Josh. Comes down to trust. Let her twist, felt her stop, pulled the trigger.

My gun was thunder, drowning out the *snap, snap* of the Tesla. The wooden upright beside Josh exploded, blown apart by the over-discharge. He cried out as flying splinters peppered the right side of his face. I saw the glass in his spectacles break.

Takes Rosie a count of three between shots.

Josh staggered, almost fell. He tore off his eye glasses and flung them in the mud. Blood on his face. He twisted round, switched gun-hand, fired.

Felt the hit; left side, above my hip. Like being kicked by a mule, even though the copper filigree in my waistcoat took most of it. Fell back on my ass in the mud. Pulled the trigger.

I hit Josh. Hit him in the left armpit, and he folded up like a busted parasol. I think he cried out, but all I could hear was the dull echo of Rosie's roar. Josh toppled into the mud and rolled over onto his back. The Tesla still pointed my way, but he didn't fire again. Couldn't keep Rosie up and let my hands drop into my lap.

The only sound was the rain.

Bert Miller jumped down into the street and knelt beside his son. He stroked Josh's cheek and gently pulled the gun from his hand—then stood and looked over. There was murder writ on his face, plain as anything.

I lifted Rosie, but her regulator was charred and smoking—she was done. And I was a dead man.

Bert Miller aimed at me. I heard the kaleidoscope whine as he dialed-up a full discharge. The containment chamber glowed.

So did Bert's eyes.

Bert Miller's head exploded as his brain flash-boiled. He didn't jerk or cry out or anything like that. Just collapsed over the body of his son, and lay still. The pink mist drifted away.

Violet Parma stood behind him, holding a Rutherford induction shotgun, price tag and all. She blinked, lowered her weapon slowly. Seemed to notice me for the first time and nodded.

I sat in the mud, feeling the burn start to hurt, the air all sharp on my tongue.

It rained. It surely did.

###

About the Author

Martin M. Clark is a freelance writer and occasional poet. He is the author of supernatural noir novellas formally produced by Eggplant Literary Productions (now sadly defunct) and short stories in Third Flatiron anthologies. He also contributes to several online publications, including Mythaxis.co.uk, Timelesstales.com, and Kraxon.com. His range of subject matter includes science fiction, urban fantasy, romance, and westerns. He puts this down to the somewhat eclectic mobile lending library where he grew up. His first novel, *Whisper My Name*, is available on Amazon.

He works as a local government officer in south-west Scotland but still finds time to be an evil stepfather.

*****~~~~~*****

The Wind Father

by Geoff Gander

"Four dead, Sergeant. All at the table," said Junior Constable Dunstan McCormick, his voice trembling.

Sergeant Henry Blake, of the North West Mounted Police, exhaled slowly. "Four? Who is missing?" he asked. The McIlroys had three children.

The dark-haired Constable wiped his brow. "I. . . there's the man and wife, and two sons. I'm sorry, Sergeant, I don't—"

Blake held up a hand. "That will do, McCormick. They also had a daughter, Clara." *The lad's still green*, thought Blake. It had taken him a while to get to know the homesteaders when he started out, after all. "Inspect the rest of the house, then go get Westler and check out the wood pile." The young man saluted and strode away shakily. Blake sagged in his saddle and rubbed his eyes. The McIlroys had invited him to dinner the first time he had been on patrol. Clara had been a baby, but even then her liveliness lit up the room like a chandelier. He hoped she had escaped. If she had, he would find her.

He rode his horse through the fields surrounding the single-storey farmhouse. Several sets of footprints, all leading east, marred the even rows of growing wheat. The closest homesteads in this part of the newly formed District of Assiniboia were a few miles to the northwest. He gazed eastwards, where the bulk of the Cypress Hills loomed over the horizon. Difficult country in more ways than one. He absently stroked the butt of his rifle slung over the saddle horn.

A flash of crimson amidst the green grass caught his eye. He dismounted and pushed aside the blood-spattered stalks to find a large patch of flattened vegetation. Drag marks led away from the patch and rejoined the tracks leading east. A clump of red hair hung limply from some half-trampled thistles. Blake's heart quickened. Clara hadn't given up without a fight, and she had at least been taken alive.

Corporal Thomas Westler approached him from the house. He nodded curtly. "The McIlroys were caught by surprise at their table," he said. "No money or valuables were taken. Just like the Donaldsons last month."

Blake narrowed his eyes and nodded, concealing a flash of irritation at Westler's informal tone.

"Their daughter is missing. I believe she was taken alive," he said. He had chatted with the family many times while on patrol. Henry and Anna were—had been, Blake corrected himself—solid, welcoming folk who knew their neighbours. They had no reason to be wary. "Mount up and return to Fort Walsh," said Blake. "These were no common criminals."

...

Blake rapped politely on the Commissioner's door. "Enter," called a voice from within. He took in a deep breath, brushed at his crimson tunic, and stepped into the spartan office. Commissioner Acheson Gosford Irvine sat at a dark wooden desk in front of an unlit fireplace. He leaned back in his plain wooden chair, regarding Blake in silence. Blake snapped a salute. Irvine nodded in acknowledgement and gestured to a ladder-back chair facing his desk. "Have you any new information on the homesteader slayings?" he asked.

"Yes, sir," said Blake, sitting. "The McIlroy homestead was indeed attacked as had been reported to us. It happened the same way as at the Donaldsons. In this case, however, one person—a daughter named Clara—has disappeared. I have reason to believe she had been abducted."

"Where did the assailants go?"

"East, towards the Cypress Hills," said Blake. "The tracks from the other site also headed in that direction, if I remember correctly from what Sergeant Thompson said. I suspect it's the work of hardened criminals from south of the border. With your permission I could take a small detachment and—"

Irvine cut him off with a wave. "Blake, I commend your dedication. However, you are proceeding on the basis of supposition. Let's not go running off on white chargers."

"Sir, even the rudest rum-runner wouldn't stoop to such a deed. Besides, the sheer savagery of the act is beyond all but the hardest madmen. Is it not our duty to keep the peace in the name of Canada and the Queen?"

"Sergeant Blake," said Irvine in an even tone, "as you know, matters are tense and our forces are stretched thin; we do not need another conflict. I will mention what you found to the local chiefs, and ask them to keep a closer watch over their lands. That will be all." He held Blake's gaze, unblinking.

"With all due respect, sir," said Blake, "there is a very good chance one of our own people, a young girl, is even now—"

"Sergeant Blake," said Irvine, rising. "We cannot go haring off to stir up trouble where none existed before. What happened to the McIlroys is horrible, but a fact of life out here. You will drop this matter immediately."

"Very well, sir," said Blake. He stood, saluted, and left the office.

...

McCormick and Westler waited outside the Commissioner's block. They snapped to attention as Blake approached. The sergeant took a deep breath. A warm breeze wafted the faint sweetness of wildflowers over the palisade. The wind shifted, bringing the odour of sweat, oiled leather, and horse dung.

"What's the word?" asked Westler.

"We are to trust the chiefs to send word," Blake said quietly. "And we will go back on patrol."

McCormick looked down at his boots. Westler adjusted his pith helmet against the sun and regarded Blake evenly. "You'll be waiting a month of Sundays for that to happen," he said. "They don't give a damned toss what happens to homesteaders."

Blake frowned. Westler was a dependable man, but other sergeants had warned him about the corporal's insouciance and outspoken manner. He had let his status as one of the "Originals"—the very first recruits—go to his head, they said. "It is in the interests of the Plains Indians to work with us, Corporal," said Blake evenly.

"If we want justice, we'll have to see to it ourselves," said Westler. "We each swore an oath when we signed up."

The ravaged homestead filled Blake's vision. Blood covered the dirt floor like a muddy carpet, while its tang hung heavy in the stifling air of the sod hut. The buttery scent of roast chicken replaced the stench of blood. Once he'd tried Mrs. McIlroy's cooking, everything else tasted like shoe leather.

"Yes, Corporal," he replied, keeping his voice steady, "each of us made an oath to uphold the law. We also have obligations towards our commanding officers. Mount up."

The business of replenishing supplies and checking the mounts provided Blake a welcome diversion from his thoughts. He smiled in satisfaction as he cinched the girdle of his horse's saddle. It was a simple task, but if done improperly could get him killed. Right or wrong; no ambiguity.

Blake regarded the green plains stretching away in all directions like an ocean under a cheerful yellow sun. The Cypress Hills loomed to the southwest. He clenched his reins. Five years ago he had been a bored bank clerk in Kingston, Ontario, whose only excitement was reading about the exploits of the Northwest Mounted Police. He had signed up as soon as the call went out for a few good men. The reality had not always lived up to the breathless accounts of adventure.

"Where to, Sarge?" asked Westler, lounging in his saddle like a cat basking in the sun. Blake had seen how quickly the corporal could snap to attention and defend himself when set upon by rum-runners.

Blake gazed towards the Cypress Hills again. *What am I doing*, he thought. He was the envy of any man back east, if the papers were any guide. Fort Walsh was a good posting, and all his needs were met. If he kept his nose clean he could retire with a tidy sum and buy some land out here. Many would say it was a lot to throw away on a matter of principle—even one of justice. The Commissioner was right; their forces were stretched thin. *But we are all there is.*

"That way," he said, pointing to the hills. "Perhaps we'll find more clues about the assailants." He nudged his horse towards the hills.

McCormick and Westler followed him.

...

"Sergeant, why are we seeing these people?" asked McCormick. "We have the trail to follow. Will they tell us anything we don't already know?"

"All of the tracks lead to the Cypress Hills, and the Plains Cree live close to there," Blake said. "We will be passing through a region claimed by them, and if there's one thing I've learned, it's that nothing happens out here without the Cree knowing about it." He spurred his horse onwards. "Whatever private business they have became ours once the murders started."

The men rode in silence until a cluster of teepees by a winding river hove into view. Dense thorn bushes lined the shore. A lone man crouched on a rock hanging halfway over the river bank. Sunlight glinted off the barrel of a rifle that lay at his side. Blake waved at the man, who raised an arm in return before scurrying up the hills.

"Some guard," muttered McCormick.

Westler poked the younger man in the shoulder. "If he'd wanted to, that man would've shot you out of your saddle already."

A lean, tanned man wearing a fringed buffalo hide cloak over a richly beaded breechclout and leggings stepped out of a white teepee to stand in front of Blake's horse. The sergeant held up his empty hands and dismounted.

"I am Maskwa, chief of this band," said the man. "My people have no quarrel with the children of the Great White Mother, but I would know your names and your reason for being here."

Blake removed his helmet and introduced himself and his companions. "We know the Plains Cree honour the treaties," he said, "and we would sit with you and talk as is proper, but the matter is urgent. Homesteaders have been murdered, and we know the men who did it passed through here on their way into the hills. Have you seen them, so that we may find them and bring them to justice?"

"The killings are the work of the Tcho-Ka," said Maskwa. "We have seen them, and we will handle them."

Blake blinked, stunned. He had never heard that name before. Westler and McCormick seemed equally puzzled. "It's gone beyond handling them, honourable chief," he said. "These people must face the law of the land, and if found guilty of murder, hang for it."

"It will be dealt with," said Maskwa. "Return to your people and be at peace."

"This is now the Great White Mother's business," said Blake. "They may have a captive."

The chief nodded slowly. "There was a young one with the band we saw. A girl with red hair. We chased them, but they were too swift and crossed the river."

Clara, thought Blake, his heart racing. *There might still be time.*

"You saw her?" said Blake. "Why did you not send men to harry them until they abandoned her?"

"We do not enter the lands of the Tcho-Ka," said Maskwa. "You have spoken plainly, and I understand your need, but the girl is lost."

Blake shook his head. "That I—we—cannot accept," he said. "Justice must be served."

"Then I ask you to sit with me so I may tell you of the Tcho-Ka, so that you may find more than tears in their hills," said Maskwa.

Exchanging glances, the men joined Maskwa in his teepee. The chief stirred the coals of his smouldering fire and tossed a small bundle of dried grass into the embers. It flared up and crumbled to ashes within seconds, releasing a smoky cloud whose spiciness prickled Blake's nose.

"Sage clears the air and sends away any spirits that may be called by what I am about to say," said Maskwa. "This land was cold and dead when my people first arrived," he said. "The Tcho-Ka were here already. They were men, yet not men, and ate of their own flesh—and ours—and we lived in fear. Then the land grew warm and the grasses came, and hunting was good. But the Tcho-Ka still ate men, and took our women and children if they could. Then the Creator came to us, and He told us the Tcho-Ka were not His children. He gave us the strength of buffalo, and we drove the Tcho-Ka into the hills, but their father was strong and would not let us kill them all. We made them swear never to wander, and we watched them. Until now."

Westler opened his mouth to say something. Blake held up his hand. "You must forgive me, honourable chief, if your tale seems strange," he said slowly. "We have never dealt with these Tcho-Ka, or even heard of them. Not even the missionaries I've met have spoken of them."

"You know the Great White Mother is real, even though you have not seen her," said Maskwa.

Blake nodded. He couldn't argue with that point. "Even so, why did your people not tell us of the Tcho-Ka?" he asked.

"Your medicine would do no better than ours against them," said Maskwa. "We have a saying—that the greatest and most courageous warrior will make peace with a hostile tribe. We have lived in balance with them for a long time, but your treaties took away much. Your settlers draw them, yet we can no longer watch all their ways and make them keep the ancient promises." He leaned back and regarded them.

"If these Tcho-Ka are as dangerous as you say, and are truly the ones who attacked our people, we will bring them to justice," said Blake.

Maskwa closed his eyes and nodded slowly. "What will happen, will happen. The Tcho-Ka are powerful. Even the Great White Mother cannot destroy them."

"I thank you for your advice, honourable chief," said Blake, "but our need is great, and we must act." He nodded deeply to Maskwa after stepping outside and signalled his men to follow him.

"What did he mean by all that, Sergeant?" asked McCormick once they had ridden out of earshot.

Blake spurred his mount. "That the Tcho-Ka are a bad lot."

...

The sun hung low in the west when they arrived on the fringes of Plains Cree territory. None of them had ever ridden this far into the Cypress Hills.

"Years back, I heard a story from a rum-runner about a part of these hills that no honest Indian would set foot in," said Westler. "I thought it was balderdash, but after seeing what happened at the homestead and hearing what the chief said, I'm starting to wonder."

"We haven't seen signs of anything passing through, except for those tracks," said McCormick, shifting in his saddle. "Even thirty miles into the plains in the height of summer, you'd see more signs of life than this. I haven't heard any birds or insects, either."

Blake cocked his head to listen. Aside from a light breeze rustling the stalks of last year's wild grasses and the limbs of the trees, all was silent. When had that happened?

"Onward," he said.

They rounded a granite dome that burst from the hillside and drew up at a shallow stream. Blake stared at the opposite bank, and turned back to his companions. Westler had dropped his reins. A look of incredulity crossed his face. McCormick, his eyes wide, had drawn back his horse.

"Sergeant, what the devil is that?" he asked in a trembling voice, pointing across the stream.

The trail they had been following continued from the other bank of the stream, where it crawled up a grey, cracked slope. The few stunted plants that had found purchase there sported limp, shrivelled leaves marred by black spots. Further from the water's edge the feeble vegetation gave way to a rolling field of grey dust and rubble broken by the occasional boulder or blackened tree that reached up from the ground like the gnarled hand.

The horses grew skittish once they set foot on the other shore. Blake's mount danced as though he had stepped on hot coals, and stopped only when the sergeant murmured reassuring words into his ear and stroked his mane.

"It was good of you to ensure our horses had extra feed, McCormick," said Blake as he studied the sickly vegetation.

"Even the air smells different, Sergeant," said McCormick. "How can any man live here?" Blake sniffed. The acrid odour of ashes, burnt vegetation, and spoiled meat hung in the air. Yet there had been no sign of it on the other bank.

"The Tcho-Ka do," said Westler. "But what that says about them. . . " his voice trailed off. They rode in silence, passing low, crumbling hills and sandy streambeds. The ground grew loose and rocky, while the landscape faded into a grey haze, through which a pale yellow sun shone faintly.

"Let's find out what we need to know and leave. I don't want to camp here," said Westler.

"The chief did say the Tcho-Ka have powerful medicine," said McCormick. "Do you think they did—this?" He gestured at the encroaching mists.

Blake peered into the gloom. "Before today I'd have sworn a place like this didn't exist. Make sure your weapons are loaded."

The terrain sloped downwards, with the ground becoming covered by patches of fine grey sand that erupted in tiny puffs wherever the horses stepped.

"I hear drums," said Westler, pointing to the right. Blake cocked his head. A series of dull, booming thuds echoed in the distance. He steered his horse towards the sound. The voices slowly grew distinct as they approached. The words were clipped and harsh, and Blake's smattering of Cree was no help in understanding any of it.

The bright orange light of a bonfire cut through the mists. As the three men drew near, the edge of a square-shaped depression resolved itself, whose shiny black floor reflected the firelight.

"Looks like it goes off a ways," said Westler in a low voice. "What kind of stone is that? It's almost like glass."

"No idea," Blake said, "but it seems to be one solid piece." He turned towards the fire. Wispy silhouettes flickered across the flame. The drumming rose to a fevered intensity. A piercing voice shouted above the din, followed by a keening wail.

"We go in openly," said Blake. The others nudged their horses to follow. The drumming faltered, then died, as the mounted policemen emerged from the mist into the light of the bonfire. Blake raised an open palm into the air. "People of the Tcho-Ka," he called out in a resonant tone, "we come in peace. We would speak with your chief."

The massed men and women before them murmured in their own sibilant language and drew back. They were shorter than the Plains Cree, and gaunt. Their skins were white as a fish's underbelly, and many sported large patches of bumps or warts that reminded Blake of a toad. He wondered what kind of sickness afflicted them. A wiry man with a shaven head and wearing a filthy fringed leather cape crept from the crowd to stand before Blake. He peered up. His large, yellow eyes reminded the sergeant of a fish's. Blake bit his lip as the stench of unwashed body and uncured hide washed over him.

"You here. Why?" asked the man in a croaking voice. He fingered a string of rawhide around his neck, from which hung bones, colourful stones, and a tarnished silver crucifix.

"Your warriors have killed the Great White Mother's children," said Blake. "She is angry, and will punish you, unless you give me the men who did these deeds."

The chief grinned, revealing teeth filed to sharp points. "Wind Father hungry. Not-brothers close the way before, but now we go through. Wind Father eat."

"What the devil is he saying?" said Westler.

Blake raised his hand. "Who is the Wind Father?" he asked.

"Wind Father bring cold and snow," said the chief. "All this," he gestured to the smudged hills faintly visible through the mists, "His land. Cold always. Not-brothers," he gestured vaguely in the direction of the Plains Cree territory, "hunt Tcho-Ka. Wind Father angry. Hungry."

"And. . . what does the Wind Father eat?" asked McCormick in a small voice.

The chief hissed words in his own language. Several men squatting in the circle sprang to their feet, revealing a gap in the circle. A pale form lay bound on the ground next to the fire, its creamy flesh missing in places, marred by precise, crimson cuts. A shock of red hair shone in the firelight. Blake's breath caught. A strangled gurgle erupted from McCormick.

"Hungry," said the gaunt man, grinning again.

"Fall back," shouted Blake as he wheeled his horse and drew his pistol. The chief shouted, his cry becoming drowned out by the deep howling of his warriors, who leaped up and banged short spears on hide shields.

A warrior emerged from the mist and jabbed a spear tipped with shiny black stone into the flank of Blake's horse as he rode past. The animal bucked, screaming. Blake fired wildly at his opponent, the crack of the discharge barely discernible over the shouting. Another crack, followed by a shriek, echoed to his left. A whiff of gunpowder filled his nostrils. He surged up the slope. Westler, surrounded by wisps of gun smoke, had stationed himself thirty feet ahead. He raised his rifle and squeezed the trigger. Smoke. Another crack. Another scream.

"They got McCormick, Sarge," he shouted.

Blake drew up next to Westler and wheeled about. He fired at a warrior who sprinted after McCormick's bloodied, riderless horse. The man grunted and pitched forward onto the stony ground, clutching his midsection.

"He's still alive," said Westler in a cracking voice, pointing towards the bonfire. Two warriors had dragged McCormick before the chief. One man kicked the constable's legs until he knelt on the ground.

A loud hiss cut through the shouting. A sudden blast of frigid air stung Blake's face and hands. The chief's voice echoed off the rock walls.

"Issa-Ka! Issa-Ka!" A thick layer of frost sprouted on the rocks. The warriors closest to the lawmen cried out and pointed at the frozen earth. Others pointed skywards, kneeling and shouting in fearful tones.

Blake glanced up. Leaden clouds hung over his head, seemingly just out of reach. The air pulsed as invisible waves bore downwards, each hitting him with a blast of cold air, slowly at first but quickly increasing in tempo. The clouds began to swirl above the bonfire in time with the unearthly beat, darkening as they did so. The chief shouted a command and pointed a knife at the mounted policemen before turning to McCormick. A band of warriors sprang up and rushed towards Blake and Westler, while the remainder formed a wall between them and their companion.

"Protect me while I get McCormick," shouted Blake. The Tcho-Ka scattered before him as he galloped down the slope. Westler's rifle cracked. A warrior crumpled to the icy ground, screaming. The chief began to sing in a grating voice and stretched his arms up to the growing cyclone above him. Green lightning flashed, followed by an icy wind that buffeted the crowd below.

Blake dug in his heels as his horse leaped over a crouching figure. Something large and hard slammed into his knee, which exploded in fiery agony. The world blurred and spun. He gripped the saddle horn and leaned forward to avoid tumbling to the frozen ground. His fingers brushed his trousers where he had been hit. Wet. Warm. Shouting in fury and pain, Blake lashed out with the butt of his pistol. His arm shuddered as his blow hit something solid. Westler fired again.

The chief's voice rose to a crescendo, then fell silent. Blake blinked away his tears and looked up. The wall of men rushed to meet him. The chief, his face flushed in ecstasy, looked down at McCormick—held down by a knot of men. With a final shout of "Issa-Ka!" the chief plunged a long, green-bladed knife into the young man's chest. As McCormick screamed, the black cyclone surged downwards, trailing wispy, writhing tendrils of smoke. Its point seemed to cave in on itself, revealing an opening that reminded Blake of a gaping maw. His hand shook as he aimed at the chief's head and squeezed the trigger.

The bullet hit a warrior who leapt before his chief, who then tumbled to the ground. His neighbours bolted, opening a gap between Blake and the chief. The gaunt man gazed skyward, smiling, and knelt beside McCormick. He placed his knife against McCormick's throat. The constable lay twitching. Bubbling blood seeped from his quivering lips.

A misty black tendril brushed the ground next to the chief. The rocky soil crackled as it froze. Another caressed a fallen warrior, whose flesh split and turned chalky white.

Blake fired.

McCormick lay still.

The chief looked up, his features frozen in terror.

A shrieking wind blasted the site of the ritual, tossing fist-sized stones like pebbles. Men screamed in terror and pain as they stumbled about. Blake shielded his eyes, gasping in agony as his flesh burned from the cold. He seized the reins with unfeeling fingers as his horse wheeled and galloped up the slope. Westler rode ahead.

He looked back at Blake, urging him on. A bright light erupted behind them. The screaming behind them acquired a fevered pitch. Blake caught up with Westler, who sat frozen in his saddle, his mouth agape.

"What is it?" asked Blake. Westler shook his head.

Blake looked back. He screamed.

...

Henry Blake rode west, towards the open arms of the Rocky Mountains. He would welcome their embrace.

"Peace, order, and good government," he muttered bitterly. The government's slogan seemed feeble on the unforgiving plains beneath a cold, endless prairie sky.

Westler had said nothing until they limped back into the Cree camp the following morning. Maskwa took them into his teepee and covered Westler with his own blankets. He did not move or speak all day. That night the corporal whispered to Blake: "He watches. He knows us." He was dead the next morning.

Blake looked skyward and shuddered. Every cloud now held icy malice, every breeze whispered threats of doom, while the sun stared down like a cold, malevolent eye. No, he would not feel safe until he stood in the shadows of the great firs of British Columbia.

He watches.

The Tcho-Ka chief, and those warriors closest to him, had stood like statues, their faces frozen in agony and terror. And statues they were, for their bodies had frozen solid in an instant, rupturing soft flesh, freezing blood, and spilling organs as they burst outwards. It was not the grisly act, but the malign presence behind it, that sent Blake fleeing. For no force of nature could entomb those men, wailing and moaning, inside their own ruined, frozen bodies.

Issa-Ka had been denied his due.

And now He knows me.

###

About the Author

Prior to writing fiction, Geoff Gander was involved in the roleplaying community and wrote many game products. His first short novel, *The Tunnelers*, was published in 2011 by Solstice Publishing. He has since been published by Metahuman Press, AE SciFi, Exile Editions, McGraw-Hill, and Expeditious Retreat Press. He primarily writes horror, but will try any genre for kicks.

Geoff is currently crafting games and stories as a member of the Sessorium of Creatives, the exclusive creative community of The Ed Greenwood Group (TEGG).

When he isn't writing or working a day job, Geoff reads, entertains his two boys, watches British comedies, and plays roleplaying games. Geoff divides his time between Ottawa and South Mountain, where a lovely stone-carving, bagpipe-playing witch resides with her many cats.

*****~~~~~*****

Etiquette for the Space Traveller: Dealing with the Ship's Cat

by Lisa Timpf

Author's note: Although ship's cats may be male or female, the pronoun "he" is used for simplicity.

Whether you're planning a simple jump to the lunar surface or gearing up for a voyage to the galaxy's farthest fringes, your voyage will be more pleasant if you familiarize yourself with shipboard etiquette—a critical aspect of which revolves around the ship's cat. Showing your savvy in dealing with these cryptic but critically important felines will go a long way toward ingratiating yourself with the crew.

Throughout Terran history, as mankind plied Earth's vast waterways, the ship's cat cruised along, performing an important role by ensuring that vessels remained rodent-free.

Now, in the twenty-second century, no self-respecting skipper of a space-faring vessel considers his roster complete without at least one ship's cat among the crew.

You must begin by understanding that all felines are endowed with a great degree (some might argue an excessive amount) of dignity. You must not condescend in any manner to a ship's cat. Refrain from referring to him as "puss" or "kitty." Rather, make it your business to learn the names of all ship's cats aboard the vessel, and you will mark yourself as a knowledgeable traveller.

Ship's cat nomenclature is a fascinating study. Some ship's cats will bear monikers derived from their famous forebears, such as Blackie, Convoy, Simon, or Unsinkable Sam. Others might be dubbed in honour of the fearless felines who manned the first interstellar colony ships—Sputnik, Starchild, Orson, Vulcan, and the like.

Names aren't the only feature the ship's cat shares with his forerunners. The keen observer will notc that today's ship's cats universally bear the trait of polydactylism, meaning the occurrence of extra toes. Sea-bound sailors observed that ship's cats with surplus digits showed superior performance when it came to climbing, maintaining balance on a wave-tossed ship, and capturing their prey. After decades of genetic manipulation, the polydactyl trait has become the standard, with ship's cats possessing as many as eight toes on each of their front feet.

If the snowshoe-like front paws strike you as odd when you first notice this feature, do not stare, and do not, on any condition, laugh. The ship's cat abhors being the butt of humour, even more than he hates being called late for dinner. Simply remember that the extra toes make the ship's cat more effective at his job: killing rodents which might otherwise spread disease, deplete food stores, or damage sensitive equipment.

The ship's cat automatically has right-of-way in any corridor or through fare. Although it is not necessary to salute, etiquette demands that you step aside when the ship's cat approaches, nodding respectfully as he passes.

Like many of today's working animals, the ship's cat is endowed with an Artificial Intelligence implant which boosts his reasoning powers. If a crew member tries to convince you that the ship's cat, resultantly, is called upon for the captain by advice, he is pulling your leg. Furthermore, the expression "putting on your thinking cat" is pure fantasy. I have yet to see a captain, even in the direst circumstances, bearing a ship's cat upon his or her head.

However, the AI implant does enable the ship's cat to readily identify all pests known to mankind, with ongoing updates downloaded as new species are discovered. As a side effect of his enhanced intelligence, the ship's cat has, in many cases, developed an obsession with the game of poker, indulging in games whenever he is not eating, sleeping or working—pursuits which, admittedly, consume the lion's share of his time. His naturally occurring inscrutable expression and razor-sharp predatory instincts make the ship's cat a formidable opponent. Unless you have a strong desire to be parted from your cash, playing high-stakes poker against the ship's cat is not recommended.

Although interrupting the ship's cat while he is on duty is frowned upon, interaction is both permitted and welcome during his down time. Even in the passenger's lounge, do not be forward with the ship's cat. Allow him to seek you out, rather than the reverse. If the ship's cat does choose to honor you with his attention, conduct yourself as though you are in the presence of royalty, and all will be well.

Above all, do not pity the ship's cat. Once introduced to the challenges and pleasures of space travel, the ship's cat never looks back.

The smoothness of any space voyage is, to a large extent, influenced by the proficiency of the ship's cat. Unfortunately, he knows this -- and he is unlikely to let you, or anyone else on board, forget it.

###

About the Author

Lisa Timpf is a freelance writer who lives in Simcoe, Ontario. Her work has appeared in a variety of venues, including *The Martian Wave, Star*Line, Outposts of Beyond, New Myths,* and *Chicken Soup for the Soul: My Very Good, Very Bad Dog.*

Lisa notes that this piece is a blend of fact (polydactylism really is a trait preferred on ship's cats; the historical ship's cat's names listed are accurate) and fantasy, taking a tongue-in-cheek view at how the ship's cat might play out in space. She has based the story in part on her experience of being "owned" by a cat for a number of years.

*****~~~~~*****

Gardening in a Post-Apocalyptic World

by Sheryl Normandeau

Media release, Portland, OR, April 5, 2047

Out this spring from Redolent Roots Press: *Gardening in a Post-Apocalyptic World*!

On the heels of the passage of monumental Bill GR08, we're delighted that the Department of Agriculture has finally given gardeners and farmers the go-ahead to get growing once again! Food production will face significant challenges over the next several decades, and we're thrilled that the inimitable Guru of Green, Devin Hurt, MSc, BSA, has written his comprehensive guide, *Gardening in a Post-Apocalyptic World*, available now through Redolent Roots Press. This indispensable volume will set the country's gardening circles on fire! (Well, not literally: been there, done that).

Former methods of gardening are obviously no longer viable, and we need the tools and knowledge to transition safely and healthily into this new era. *Gardening in a Post-Apocalyptic World* extensively covers all of the topics eager gardeners are itching to learn, and—as his readers have come to expect—Devin Hurt's wisdom is fresh, frank, and accessible.

Here is Mr. Hurt on the topic of soil microbes:

Our soils have been stripped of all nutrients and biological essences, and in many locations, are contaminated by radioactive elements. A couple of years ago, composted manure could fix just about any soil issue—but now, a bag or two of shit just doesn't cut it. You need to rebuild the entire soil microcosm from the ground up, and coax out a nice loamy base for your delicious vegetables. Fortunately, the federal government has stepped in and manufactured the required complex microbes in laboratories all over the country. Contrary to those news reports out of Wisconsin, Microbial Mix[TM] has caused grievous facial and upper body injuries to only one technician, not fourteen as initially suggested, but it may be prudent to keep children and pets indoors during application. Always wear protective clothing to reduce the risk of losing digits, eyes, or other important body parts. I can confidently testify that the microbes become less aggressive when placed in contact with the soil, and the doctors say that with enough radiation exposure, the tip of my pinky will eventually grow back.

His valuable take-away about genetically engineered plants:

If you were worried about genetically engineered food before the apocalypse—the fact that these biological freaks might insinuate themselves into your diet or somehow cross-breed with your heirloom tomatoes or beans—you don't have to worry any longer. You have absolutely no choice in the matter. Because the impenetrable seed banks were found to be as fallible as their human creators, we're SOL on the old, treasured seed varieties. You're stuck with genetically engineered plants, so suck it up. Don't even get me started on organic gardening. But don't fear—I will teach you everything you need to know about successfully growing from GE seed. In no time at all, you'll be delighting in the scrumptious crunch of a 'Fluorglow' carrot, flavored with the terroir of soils enriched by Microbial Mix. Nothing like fresh veggies and fruits for your family and soon, the nation!

And Mr. Hurt's advice for those extremely difficult landscape features:

When hellstrip gardening has truly gone to hell, you need a shot of creativity. Scorched earth can look mighty fine when dressed up with decorative containers brimming with leafy greens—plus, you can practice cut-and-come-again and eat the plants when your rations run low at the end of the month. (That is, if the mutant squirrels don't get to them first—see Chapter 7 for my zesty pest annihilation tips). Gardening in a post-apocalyptic world is all about sustainability, but there is no reason it can't look seriously swanky at the same time!

More Information

Help us spread the word about *Gardening in a Post-Apocalyptic World* by requesting your media kit now. If you would like to interview Mr. Hurt, contact me, and I will be happy to make the arrangements.

Penny Dervish, Redolent Roots Press, penny@redolent.endtimes.ex.

###

About the Author

Sheryl Normandeau is a Calgary-based writer whose short stories have been published in numerous anthologies, including Third Flatiron's *Universe Horribilis.*

*****~~~~~*****

The JPEG of Dorian Gray

by Brian Trent

The city was long gone, but the fire hydrants remained, rising from the bog like oversized mushrooms. They were cast iron, after all, unlike the wood and stone and steel that had rotted and crumbled and rusted with the passage of centuries. Cast iron, even slowly eaten by corrosion, had outlasted them all.

Like him.

"But not nearly as pretty as me," Dorian Gray muttered, looking around.

The hydrants rose from a vile green marshland that had him ankle-deep in brackish water and duckweed. The mud sucked at his boots as he pressed deeper into the territory. Trees bent sorrowfully to the water, echoing in their way Caravaggio's oil-on-canvas of Narcissus gazing lovingly at his own reflection.

Dorian stared, his pale and lovely face marred by dark thoughts.

No, he thought. Not like Narcissus. These trees were gnarled and crooked things, bent like craggy hags to consider their equally horrendous reflections. There was no love in that mirroring. And the trees were rotting: these were white oaks and sycamores from the *old* days, not yet evolved to deal with the area's flooding. The putrid water was turning their rooted bases to mush, resulting in this arthritic stoop.

Dorian Gray closed his eyes.

He could *feel* his picture nearby.

For the last several months he had tracked it, like the narrator in Poe's "The Tell-Tale Heart" pursuing a distant heartbeat. He knew he was closing in now. It lay somewhere in this swamp that had once been. . . Florida? No, Florida had been swallowed by the sea around 2137. Or had that been 3127? It was difficult keeping track, as the old tea parties and costumed balls and orgies aboard million-dollar yachts had expired, just as mankind had expired. The last calendars had rotted off their hangings long ago.

Except for me, Dorian Gray thought. I shall never age, and never die.

As long as the cursed picture endured.

...

The portrait that preserved him, soaking in his sins and age and injury, had been painted by Basil Hallward in 1890 in a London studio. Yet it was the fall of 1923 when Dorian decided to relocate his belongings—including the portrait—to New York.

He'd grown weary of Europe, and was enticed by the promise of novelty across the pond. Drawn by the dazzle and wealth and Jazz Age glitter, the flapper parties and bathtub gin, he'd hopped a steamer, his possessions stored in the ship's hold.

Upon arrival, Dorian went searching for the nearest speakeasy, wasting no time in getting a lay of his new land. But he was in the midst of drinking a Pink Lady, surrounded by the fawning attentions of men and women in a Lower Manhattan club, when he felt an inexplicable heat on his face.

It wasn't from the alcohol.

Dorian excused himself and dashed into the street, following the mysterious sensation. His eyes lit when he spied the harbor ablaze. A drunk sailor's improperly discarded cigarette might have started it, but Dorian ran in full-blown terror, choking and stumbling in the smoke and flames, to rescue the *one* belonging of his that could not be allowed to perish.

By the time he retrieved it and escaped the fiery vessel, it was only heat-singed around the lacquered frame.

It had been a dreadfully close call. Dorian, with soot on his cheeks, promised himself to never keep all his immortal eggs in one basket again.

The very next day, he hauled the painting to a local photographer. At Dorian's insistence, the man stood before the demonic and withered and monstrous painting and produced three high-quality tintype replicas.

In 1974 in Mexico City, Dorian purchased a Polaroid and snapped an additional photo, keeping it in his wallet.

In 2007, in a Beijing sky-rise among China's nouveau riche, he snorted cocaine from between a whore's thighs and got an idea. He fetched the laminated Polaroid, aimed his smartphone, snapped a digital picture.

And uploaded it to the Internet.

...

Dorian Gray stumbled over submerged roots and cried out, nearly breaking his ankle underwater. His cry echoed spectacularly through the trees. Scaly birds, startled by the sound of a human voice, leapt from their roost and splashed into the safety of the water as a solid black mass.

He sneered at the ripples they had left. Ugly things, he thought. Bastard children that had squeezed through evolution's birth canal.

"Nothing's as pretty as me!" he shouted in his best Southern drawl.

The hairs on his arm stood up.

Dorian stared, spying a moss-covered cave where the scaly birds had been. Vines draped across its mouth.

His picture was in there.

He could *feel* it.

Dorian splashed forward with new eagerness, trembling despite the humidity. He waded the putrid water into the cave's mouth. His feet touched a series of tiered stones.

He froze, pulse quickening in his neck.

Stairs!

Nearly blind in the gloom, Dorian climbed the stairs to a drier elevation. He passed suspiciously geometric shapes. His hand ran along slimy rocks, and he grinned bleakly when he perceived a placard illuminated through a small crack in the cave's ceiling. The words were faded but readable:

OLICE DEPART ENT
SHREVEPORT ARC LOGY
LEV L 51

Ah!

The Shreveport Arcology, established between the immigrations of the Polynesian diaspora and the Red Plague of 5430. Or had it been 5043?

Dorian hesitated.

A magnetic sensation cloyed at him, like the mud that had suckled his boots.

He felt around and found what must have been an ancient police evidence locker. Prying it apart with his hands, he located a perfectly sealed plastic bag. Then he retraced his steps into the swamp and examined what he had found by the failing daylight.

A plastic bag.

And inside?

An ancient wristphone, containing a forgotten person's emails and contact lists and. . .

Photos!

Dorian's impulsive decision to upload his demonic portrait to the world web had resulted in the hideous picture being shared and posted and saved a million times over, all across the world. His original painting could be destroyed (and he had destroyed it), and the tintype plates could be shattered (and he had shattered them) and the Polaroid burned (and he had burned it), but his immortality would go on.

On and on. . . and dreadfully, horrifically, unendingly, *on.*

Unless I can destroy every last one of them!

Dorian was sick and trembling as he reached the shore, the wristphone in his white-knuckled grip.

Something howled in the forest.

Heart hammering, he quickly placed the wristphone upon a rock. He hefted another rock and held it aloft, praying to anyone who would listen.

Over the millennia, most computer devices had corroded, their memory storage vanishing forever. But things had a way of preserving, the way fossil hunters sometimes discovered flint axes and arrowheads from Neolithic man.

And if he ever wanted to die, he needed to obliterate them all.

More howls erupted from the woods. A pack of dark shapes scrambled through the bush, drawn to his scent.

Dorian nearly gibbered with panic and the agony of hope.

He brought the rock down, over and over, pulverizing the device down to its microchip. Over and over and over.

Let!

Me!

Die!

When the wild dogs found him, he had no strength to flee them. They erupted from the woods in a slavering pack, eyes burning with hunger. In the absence of humanity, dogs had utterly shed their domesticated traits. They had returned to the dire wolf, maybe. Larger, shaggier, with serrated teeth like stilettos in frothy mouths.

Dorian spread his arms and let them have him.

It was a bad way to die. Always was.

You heard them chewing and cracking your bones.

…

Something tickled his face.

He opened his eyes to find flies crawling and buzzing about his bloodied body. The nightmare day had folded into a lonely, cloudy, moonlit evening.

Dorian Gray jerked to his feet. The dogs were gone, their bellies fat with his flesh. The ground was sticky and reeked of carnage. His bloodied clothes were shredded, hanging like graveyard cerements from lank limbs.

His wounds, however, had entirely healed.

As they always did.

Dorian gazed up at the crescent moon, as if seeking mercy from its cold and leering gaze. The flies alighted on the blood that had dried on his face and neck.

A soft vibration suddenly tingled his neck, like the hand of a ghostly lover.

There was a picture of him somewhere to the west.

Dorian Gray stood, legs rubbery, stomach grumbling for food. He took two steps in the direction of the magical beckoning. Then he collapsed to his knees by the marsh's shore.

He gazed into the water.

The moonlight drew his reflection on its black surface. In hues of silver and shadow, he regarded his bloodied face, his mangled clothes and wild hair, and the haunted emptiness of his eternal eyes.

"Nothing's as pretty as me," he whispered, and kept staring at the reflection even as the clouds began to rain.

###

About the Author

Brian Trent's work appears in *ANALOG, Fantasy & Science Fiction, Orson Scott Card's Intergalactic Medicine Show, Daily Science Fiction,* and numerous year's-best anthologies.

*****~~~~~*****

Credits and Acknowledgments

Cover image and design – Keely Rew
Podcast production – Andrew Cairns
Readers – Keely Rew, Andrew Cairns, Tom Parker, Leonard Sitongia
Editor and Publisher – Juliana Rew

*****~~~~~*****

Discover other titles by Third Flatiron:

(1) Over the Brink: Tales of Environmental Disaster
(2) A High Shrill Thump: War Stories
(3) Origins: Colliding Causalities
(4) Universe Horribilis
(5) Playing with Fire
(6) Lost Worlds, Retraced
(7) Redshifted: Martian Stories
(8) Astronomical Odds
(9) Master Minds
(10) Abbreviated Epics
(11) The Time It Happened
(12) Only Disconnect
(13) Ain't Superstitious
(14) Third Flatiron's Best of 2015
(15) It's Come to Our Attention
(16) Hyperpowers
(17) Keystone Chronicles

www.thirdflatiron.com

Made in the USA
San Bernardino, CA
08 August 2018